G J Griffiths is a retired science teacher, with some early working experience of the photographic industry, who greatly enjoys being a grandad. Born in the UK, he enjoys reading most genres of fiction, such as sci-fi, crime/detective thrillers, historical and wildlife stories. Non-fiction reading mainly includes scientific or historical books. Walking in the English, Scottish or Welsh countryside with binoculars, ready for bird-watching or other wildlife is a particular pleasure. Seeing badgers and otters in the wild recently was an exciting first.

His first novel was *Fallen Hero.* The *So What!* series of three books followed and these are all focussed around the fictitious Birch Green High School. They include: book 1, *So What! Stories or Whatever!*; book 2, *So What's Next!*; and book 3, *So What Do I Do?*. Each book is quite different in its overall context, e.g., a collection of the teachers' experiences; the creation of a school nature corner; and arson, fraud and murder investigated by Detective Shantra, an ex-pupil from BGHS!

More recent works include poetry: *Dizzyrambic Imaginings*; two illustrated children's sci-fi stories about ant-sized aliens, *Ants in Space* and *They're Recycling Aliens*; and this historical fiction based upon real characters from the Industrial Revolution period, called *The Quarry Bank Runaways*.

If you enjoy reading one of G J Griffiths' books, please share your enjoyment with other readers and post a review of it on Amazon, etc. This is very helpful for new writers and he would be pleased to hear from you on the comments page at his website:
https://www.gjgriffithswriter.com

Dedication

To my wife, Judith, with thanks for her patience, ideas and encouragement throughout this project.

G J Griffiths

THE QUARRY BANK RUNAWAYS

AUSTIN MACAULEY PUBLISHERS™

LONDON • CAMBRIDGE • NEW YORK • SHARJAH

A CIP catalogue record for this title is available from the British Library.

ISBN 9781788486507 (Paperback)
ISBN 9781788486514 (Hardback)
ISBN 9781528954648 (ePub e-book)

www.austinmacauley.com

First Published (2019)
Austin Macauley Publishers Ltd
25 Canada Square
Canary Wharf
London
E14 5LQ

Acknowledgements

- Members of staff at Quarry Bank Mill and Alkestis Tsilika in particular: The Archive and Collections Manager.
- Swelling Grounds: A History of Hackney Workhouse 1729–1929 by Jean-Paul Martinon.
- From Smuggling to Cotton Kings by Michael Janes.
- The Industrial Revolution 1760–1830 by T S Ashton.
- Poverty and Public Health by Rosemary Rees.
- The Workshop of the World by J D Chambers.
- Beta-readers: Christine McBryde, Anne Rogers, Patricia Walker.
- The Real Oliver Twist by John Waller.
- Cover design: John Constable's 1816 painting of Flatford Mill.

Table of Contents

Foreword

In the year 1806, two apprentices, Thomas Priestley and Joseph Sefton, ran away from Quarry Bank Mill in Styal, Cheshire. It appears from archive evidence that they took about a week to walk to London and that Thomas had lost part of a finger in an accident in the cotton mill. The two runaways were later caught and brought before magistrates in a Middlesex court where they each gave detailed statements in their defence. This information remains as one of the best primary sources about life in the mill and the place where they lived with dozens of other young workers—known as the Apprentice House. Their statements gave much information about the food and clothing provided, together with details of dormitory sleeping arrangements and a little about the working duties expected from apprentices.

When I first read transcripts of these examinations, I was intrigued, my curiosity immediately led me to ask some obvious questions—questions such as: How did two young boys manage to 'walk' all that way, some 200 miles, to London? What happened to them on their journey? Did they receive any help or were they relentlessly pursued? What happened during the weeks they were in Hackney before they were caught?

To borrow a term taken from the textile industry, particularly cotton manufacture, the story you are about to read is one woven purely from my fantasising answers to those questions. While the strong warp threads are laid using Thomas' and Joseph's transcripts the weft yarn is that totally found using my imagination. I hope that the finished cloth, the final fabric of the tale, is one which you find both interesting and entertaining. You will have to forgive me if some of the added embroidery occasionally surprises or startles you. It had the same effect on the author.

There is a glossary at the end of the book to hopefully explain some of the less familiar words and terms.

Child apprentices in very many cotton mills continued to be treated like slaves well after the Slave Trade Acts of the early 19th century.

Rameau de Cotonnier
(branch of cotton plant)

Gousse de Coton ouverte
(open cotton seed pod)

Prologue

By way of an introduction to the story about Thomas and Joseph that follows I have decided to use a series of direct quotes from the excellent biography of Robert Blincoe, written by the historian John Waller. Between the ages of four and seven Robert Blincoe lived in a workhouse and, in his seventh year, was also sent 200 miles north to work in a cotton mill. The book was published in Australia and the UK in 2005, under the title 'The Real Oliver Twist', and is highly recommended. Like so many children of those times Thomas and Joseph would have been transported by stage wagon, from the workhouse where they spent their very early years, to the cotton mill of their prospective employer, many miles away. The descriptions within these quotes will give the reader a vivid textual illustration of the kind of journey that our two apprentices may have experienced for several days before they eventually arrived at Quarry Bank Mill.

"The children clambered onto the two large wagons. Those who knew anything at all about transport – and the children had seen hundreds of horse-drawn vehicles from the workhouse windows – would have realised that these were not the preferred conveyances of gentlemen or ladies. Like nearly everything else in Georgian life, mode of transport reflected wealth and status. The stately carriage drawn by four plumed and liveried horses was the hallmark of the extremely rich. Those without their own stables but with plenty of money tended to travel by post chaise; faster than stagecoaches, these held two passengers, and a post-boy rode one of the two horses. Next came stagecoaches, or diligences. These were pulled by two or four horses and had internal seating for four or, less comfortably, six passengers."

"Travellers on a budget generally went by stage wagon. This was the type of vehicle that picked up Blincoe and the 29 other work'us apprentices. Covered by canvas or leather hoods, with long benches either side, and pulled at a lethargic two miles per hour by around eight horses, stage wagons were no more than large carts. Their one advantage, aside from cheap fares, was that highwaymen kept away, most of them assuming that the passengers would be too poor to be worth fleecing."

It was most unlikely that stage wagons had efficient, if any, suspension at all but it was highly probable that the wagons carrying the unsuspecting apprentices had wooden hoods with entrance doors that could be locked. "Once these doors had been closed and bolted from the outside, the children were held within like cattle."

"On late-18th-century roads, a journey, of any considerable length, was no light undertaking. Even for those able to travel in style, road journeys could be wretchedly uncomfortable. Many turnpikes remained deeply rutted and impassable in heavy rains. Surveyors of the highways were usually parish appointees, often utterly ignorant of the science of road construction and negligent in their duties."

"The constant jolting as the heavy wheels passed over ruts and rubble induced nausea among the workhouse children and caused severe bruising as they were flung repeatedly from bench to floor. Then, in the limited light that penetrated the wooden hood, they had to struggle to regain their place."

"Few of the children had travelled in a coach before, but the sense of novelty would not have long survived the hours they spent crammed inside. In large towns, at least, they were turned out to walk. They had no difficulty in keeping up with the lumbering pace of the wagon. Blincoe remembered passing through St Albans and then Leicester, which means that they started off along Watling Street, the old Roman road."

"Although sleep was taken on the move, it still took three long and excruciating days to reach the town of Nottingham." This would have been Robert Blincoe's eventual destination as it was where Richard Lambert and his sons, William and Francis, had their hosiery business and warehouse.

Unfortunately for Thomas and Joseph their destination, of Styal in east Cheshire, would have been at least another 30 miles of bruised discomfort further on, into the north-west of England. We are told by John Waller that the children's new masters,

William and Francis Lambert, later inspected them, even browbeating them with a harsh "lecture on the sin of idleness and the duty of hard work". Whether the newly indentured children arriving at Styal received a similar welcome is not known but the Gregs were considered to be more humanitarian in their attitude towards their workers, notwithstanding they had profit at the forefront of their minds at most times.

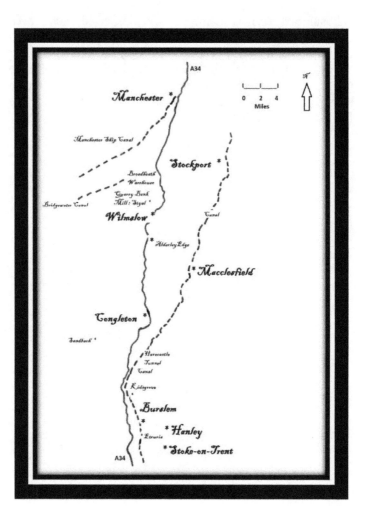

The Quarry Bank Runaways
1806

Quarry Bank Mill clock & bell tower (2016)

Quarry Bank Mill beside the River Bollin (2016)

The Apprentice House (2016)

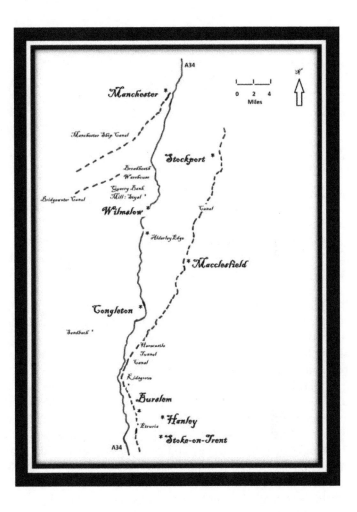

Chapter 1
Mills Apart

"Tommy, Tommy, wake up. Wake up, will you?"

"Uh! What! What is it, Joe? I was dreaming of a great big pudding and—"

"Sh! Keep your voice down, Pal. Never mind that pudding. There's two masters a-coming along the road on horseback. Let's get behind this bush afore they see us."

"Why we got to hide again, Joe?"

Without bothering to reply to his younger companion, Joseph Sefton grabbed him by the arm and pulled him into the ditch behind an overgrown hedge of hawthorn and ivy. The sleepy lad winced with pain as he hung on to his sack of meagre belongings, ensuring that he kept it with him.

"Shush," hissed Joseph. "They're here now."

He had one arm around Thomas Priestley's shoulders and also hung desperately on to his sack with his other hand. As if they were one person, the pair of boys flattened themselves into the tangle of rotting leaves and mud, ignoring the odour of stagnation that crept into their clothes and lungs. For a few minutes, the two were relieved of the stench while they held their breath, watching the gentlemen riders slowly pass by, their thoroughbred steeds huffing and puffing, eager to show their galloping prowess. The two men had much to speak of together, about gambling debts and the finer points of their newly purchased hunting hounds, so were quite unaware of the poorly dressed observers. Thomas waited until the riders were out of sight and beyond earshot for his grumbling remark.

"What we got to hide from the likes o' them gents for, Joe? We ain't done nothing wrong to them, have we?" He held his hurting hand to his chest and added, "This hand's a grieving me something terrible now."

"We just got to be careful, Tommy, tha knowst. If we get picked up and sent to the magistrate, then who knows what old Greg'll do to us for running away. I keep telling you, Pal, they got indentures on us both and running away is breaking the law."

Thomas had started to weep in his pain and frustration and was picking at the grubby cotton rag wrapped around the remains of his left forefinger. The doctor back at Quarry Bank Mill who had attended to Thomas had packed the bloody stump with a bread dough and iodine poultice of his own concoction. Hannah Greg, the wife of the mill owner, had nursed him for a short while. Despite this attention, the constant throbbing and pain meant that Thomas needed his mother and he persisted in telling anyone near to him. His friend, Joe, also from the mill, had agreed to take him along since he was bound south himself. At 17 years of age, Joseph was confident of the way to London from North Cheshire, having noted a few landmarks on his wagon journey from Hackney, some eight years earlier. When he had been the same age as Thomas, four years ago, he had accompanied one of the engineers to Sandbach to collect some parts for a spinning-mule and considered himself a seasoned traveller.

But for now, he had to raise his friend's spirits again and took Thomas' injured hand in his, saying, "I don't think you should pick at it, Pal. Doctor Holland and Mrs Greg told you to leave it for a couple of days. They said it would pain thee."

"Aye, but it's been a few weeks since."

The two boys were a sorry sight standing together on the Old Chorley road. Their cheap and well-worn clothing was wet and muddy and they had soggy brown leaves sticking to their hair and skinny legs. It was late in June but their soaked breeches, of a dubious colour, and the early morning chilly air combined to remind them of the foul, cold, ditch water. Completely distracted for a few minutes by poor Thomas' plight, they failed to notice a drover wagon slowly approaching.

"Eh up, lads! As tha fallen into the ditch then? If'n tha wants a lift you best hop on the back o' the cart... Whoa!"

The red-faced farmer, hiding behind a bush of a brown beard, stopped his wagon and looked round at the full sacks he was carrying. His enormous grin and twinkling eyes calmed the panic that had jumped to the throats of the boys.

"Are you going to Sandbach, Sir?" asked Joseph.

"Nay, lad, just to Chorley. As far as Alderley Corn Mill wi' this lot."

Thomas' teeth were chattering now; the cold having reached his bones and the pathetic sight of the boys touched the farmer's heart. They nodded to each other.

"Thank you, Sir. Much obliged," said Joseph.

"You look as though you could do with a hot drink and a visit to a wash-tub, as well as a lift. Hop on them sacks, lads. They calls me, Parbold... Gidyup, Feather!'

The enormous grey carthorse ceased sampling the long grasses at the roadside, chuffed his breath, as if responding to Parbold, then set off in its strong and steady fashion.

***

"You see, Lad, if you want to get on the road to London, you're best heading for Congleton first. Then that will lead you on to the old Roman road they calls Watling Street. But that's a way off yet. After Congleton and Stoke, you've got to reach an old village my old dad used to call Chenet."

Parbold had been talking to one of the corn millers about the boy's destination. Miller Bawtry was giving Joseph the benefit of his knowledge while he and Thomas sat around a brazier in the courtyard of Alderley Mill. Each of the boys held items of their mud-free clothing, grasped in their mud-free hands, making use of the brazier's heat to dry them. A few buckets of cold water and a block of carbolic soap had been applied to their scrawny bodies and ragged clothes, while spare flour sacks and string helped the lads retain their modesty. The sacking did little to keep them warm-up but Bawtry's wife had given the shivering pair a mug of hot tea each, for which they persisted in thanking any of the three adults who were near. The miller thought for moment before continuing.

"But now it's called summat like Canoc, and I hear there's new work there. They're setting up a coal mine nearby, as I heard it told. That's your best bet, I reckon cus the hamlet sits itself right on that old Roman road, see."

"And you both are bound for London, you say. To see your mothers, according to Parbold?'

Mrs Bawtry, a very jolly, motherly woman, was interested to hear more from the reticent teenagers. When asked from where they came, they'd answered, "Manchester," and that was all they would say. It was she who, earlier, had insisted on them getting cleaned up and staying long enough to drink the tea, and then breakfast on two enormous hunks of bread and butter.

"No, no," she had said, "you can't go on your journey looking like a right pair of scruffy ruffians. People will be watching their pockets and purses, otherwise, whenever they sees you two a-coming... You're not running from the constables, are you?"

They shook their heads and when Thomas had insisted on parting with a few of his hard-earned farthings, in return for the food and the flour sacks, she had laughed and was tempted to believe them. She asked if she might examine his injured hand with such tenderness and attention that Thomas was reminded of his mother, and he failed to hold back his tears again. At that moment, a great giant of a floury young man emerged from the mill and overheard the conversation.

He was Jonty, the eldest son of the Bawtrys, and he suggested axle grease.

"You recall, Mother, when I near pulled my thumb off a couple o' years back, when I was trying to shift that old millstone? And old Widow Chambers plastered my hand up with axle grease to keep the dirt out of the wound?"

"Well, she ain't around no more—mores the pity," said his father.

"No, but there's plenty of axle grease still in the tub," said Jonty, wiggling the thumb of his right hand and displaying a stark white chevron around the base of the digit. "Look—it's fine now."

"What dost think, Tommy? I got plenty clean pieces o' cotton I could replace that dirty scrap with." Mrs Bawtry's kind smile and gentle way about her caused his heart to flutter. A thought of returning to the corn mill, if they failed to find their mothers, flickered through his mind, such a paucity of kindness had touched the apprentices' short lives.

Jonty let out a deep bubbling chuckle and said, "It didn't do me no harm, Pal. Thee says it's hurting any road."

Thomas looked to his friend, Joseph, and then peered through squinting eyes at the floury titan. Joseph felt it was right to say, "It's up to you, Tommy. You've already lost your finger and it might stop thee losing your hand."

Thomas nodded at Mrs Bawtry and she reached out and gently patted his cheek before going inside the house, while Jonty went to fetch the tub of grease. Thomas quickly wiped the back of his good hand across his face, brushing away the tears that stung the corners of his eyes.

An hour later, Joseph and Thomas were saying farewell to their unexpected new friends. The kindness shown to them had helped dispel some of the doubts and fears they had each carried, deep down inside, for the first day of the journey from Quarry Bank Cotton Mill. For the majority of their lives, they had lived in the mill's apprentice house, eating and sleeping there when they were not working long hours, scavenging and piecing, in the cotton mill. Setting out on this second day gave them both new heart and a stronger sense of adventure and freedom, the feeling they'd hoped for at the very beginning. Not everyone, during the coming days, would show them the same level of consideration and generosity as Parbold and the Bawtrys but spirits were high that day.

Joseph was feeding Feather from a large leather bag of oats he held under the carthorse's nose. Reaching up, he patted the powerful neck and muttered words of goodbye to the horse. Thomas was near, his sack over his shoulder, with thin wisps of steam rising from the still damp clothes in which he now stood. His left hand was bound in clean white linen from which protruded his two smallest fingers. The two millers had returned to their tasks inside leaving Mrs Bawtry and Parbold to wish the boys luck on their way to London.

"Ready to go, Joe? Only it's a long walk we've got ahead of us, Pal." His boy soprano voice contrasted suddenly with the manly baritone of his friend's reply.

"Aye, Tommy, I'm ready, Mate." He turned to farmer Parbold. "You've been very good to us, Sir. Thank you again, and thank you, Mrs Bawtry. Specially fixing up Tommy's hand. No doubt Doctor Holland did a good job on it but, if Tommy grows as big as Jonty, one day… Well, we'll know who to thank, eh."

"Best o' luck, Lad," said Parbold, slapping him on the shoulder with a bear-like paw. "Now be on your way and make good time while ye can…"

Mrs Bawtry interrupted him, "This Doctor Holland, Joe, you never said where he was from. Is it Wilmslow?"

Still very wary and now more eager than ever to be on their way, Joseph said, "You'll have to excuse me if I don't answer that question, Ma'am. It's better you don't know, see. Then you won't attract any trouble to yourselves because o' what we…"

"Parbold, why do you call him Feather? He's such a big strong animal—nothing like a feather at all." Thomas cut in quickly, trying to change the subject. The farmer took the hint straight away, not wanting to put them in a corner and suspecting that Thomas got his injury while working at a cotton mill, somewhere. He answered just as quickly.

"Ah, now then, that there's a good question, Lad. He was a cross, see—not planned—but through a frisky Old English Black what jumped a hedge into the field with my grey mare. When he were born, the poor mare needed a lot o' help foaling, and out comes this scrap of a colt. I had to carry him to another stall, see, cus his mother was in a bad way… Light as a feather, he were."

"Did she die—his mother?" asked Joseph.

"Aye, Lad, eventually she did. But it took a while and I was all for giving the foal and mother to the knackers as well… But Mrs Parbold is like Mrs here," he nodded towards the miller's wife. "Too soft-hearted, see, and she and Widow Chambers fed him up when he were suckling, on goat and cow's milk… Hee, hee." Parbold could not resist a chuckle. "The two women called him Feather all along his suckling, see. So, we called him Feather… Aye, rum do, eh? Look at him now. Best horse I ever put to a dray. Eh up, Feather, Lad, don't get too fat on all them oats. We got work to do."

The horse took his nose out of the bag of oats and whinnied, snuffling and bobbing his enormous proud head up and down at his friend and master. The affection between them was unmistakeable. Joseph walked across to Thomas, grinning. He gently took hold of his companion's injured hand and waved it at Parbold and Mrs Bawtry.

"I reckon there's a good chance my mate, Tommy, might follow in Feather's path and grow as big as your son, Mrs Bawtry. I suspect there's something in the water round here."

"Aye, well they do say that about the River Bollin, tha knowst," retorted Parbold, laughing.

At the mention of the River Bollin, the eyes of the two apprentices met, slight alarm showing in their faces. It disappeared when they went to shake Parbold's hand and endured an embarrassing, but affectionate, hug from Mrs Bawtry. Then they were on their way, striding out south to Beartown, Congleton.

***

Thomas Priestley had had his accident a few weeks before setting out on their journey to London. While disentangling cotton thread from a spinning machine, his finger had been severed by one of the steel wheels, since it was not the practice to turn it off once running. Disentangling cotton thread from moving machinery in order to piece together the broken ends was a very risky business. If the child was too tired to pay proper attention to the task in hand then cut or broken fingers often resulted.

It was while he was working as an apprentice to Samuel Greg, the owner of Quarry Bank Cotton Mill at Styal in Cheshire. Both boys had been housed there as indentured child apprentices. A few years earlier, Thomas, with a group of other children, had been taken there from the Hackney workhouse where he had been living with his mother. The destitute mother and child had been sent to the workhouse after the death of his father, a turnkey of Newgate Prison.

Joseph Sefton was born in Clerkenwell, around 1790, and had been deserted by his father, during his son's second year of life, when he'd enlisted as a soldier. A year later, Joseph was also taken into Hackney workhouse and later still, around the age of nine, he too became a bound apprentice to Quarry Bank Mill. The place of work for the two youngsters was to be about two hundred miles north of their birthplace. Like many of the workhouse children apprenticed to Samuel Greg's cotton mill, Joseph was a sickly child, of stunted growth for his age but determined to survive to adulthood. He, too, desired to see his mother, having been suffering from 'ill humours of the bowel' for a while, at the time of Thomas' injury.

Stomach complaints were not uncommon amongst the young apprentices since many of them were too exhausted after working for an hour or more, first thing in the morning, to wash their hands for breakfast. It was doubtful they had the opportunity as their usual water pump stood outside the door of the apprentice house several hundred yards away. Apprenticed workers had to rise at five-thirty to start work at six, which usually meant scrabbling on the mill floor as scavengers or handling oily machinery and equipment with other tasks, such as mule doffing and can tenting. Stopping to receive breakfast they would hold out a grubby hand, into which was ladled a solid lump of cold porridge that would glue dust and oil to itself before being hungrily consumed by the drowsy worker.

Very few of the youngsters would feel inclined to approach the Greg's physician more than once for something 'to settle their stomachs' in the form of a large soup spoonful of brimstone and treacle. Quite apart from the painful motions coursing around their lower abdomen, causing urgent races to the privy, they also stood to lose wages or attract fines from failing to be at their expected place of work later in the day.

Although Joseph had asked for some time off from his work at the mill, so that he could see his mother, he had been refused. But his heart ached to see his mother again and he was determined to go. He reckoned that by sticking to the bigger roads used by sheep and cattle drovers, and following the smaller pack-horse routes in between, he could find his way south to Hackney. Thomas begged to be taken along as well and his pal agreed if he could pay his own way. When a hardware delivery man from Chorley confirmed to Joseph there were main livestock markets in Kidsgrove, Stoke and Stafford along the way, he felt certain they would make it.

"You see, Tommy, I reckon if we can get as far as Stafford, or thereabouts, we'll be half-way to London. So, after a couple more days on the road we'll be there, Mate."

"I've got a bit of money put aside from my cobble collecting, Joe, and we can get a couple of lifts if we're lucky."

"And there's canals going south now I hear, Tommy, so who knows, eh? It could be we'll get a ride on a barge for a couple o' miles."

So, with some enthusiasm and a lot of apprehension, the two waited for the right moment to slip away from the Mill. Within three days of their departure, they were to discover just how much further on their journey to London they would be than Joseph's rough 'half-way' point. Their brief escape from the tedium and hard work of their daily labours would include many more towns. Congleton, Stone, Tamworth, Atherstone, Towcester and Dunstable would all be providing the young men with unexpected challenges and experiences days before they arrived at the outskirts of England's capital city.

A34

Manchester *

Manchester Ship Canal

Stockport *

Broadheath
Warehouse

Quarry Bank
Mill: Styal *

Bridgewater Canal

Canal

Wm Wilmslow *

* Alderley Edge

* Macclesfield

Congleton *

'Sandbach'

Harecastle
Tunnel
Canal

Ridgeove

Burslem

* Hanley

* Etruria

* Stoke-on-Trent

A34

N

0   2   4
Miles

Chapter 2
Turnpikes to Beartown

Richard Sims, the superintendent of the apprentice house at Quarry Bank Mill, was not happy that two of his charges had slipped out under cover of darkness. He blamed his wife as usual, who was adamant that when she had counted heads in bed that Saturday night, in both the boys' and girls' dormitories, it had tallied. When Mrs Sims had locked the door to the boys' gloomy room, she had given it a cursory glance, being in a hurry to finish the starching of the girls' clean mop caps and aprons ready for the weekly visit to St Bartholomew's Church on Sunday. Supervising the girls while they patched up elbows and knees on some of the boys' Sunday clothes had not gone well; so many of the new girls had not 'the faintest idea about going about it all'. Showing them had taken up most of her afternoon and all of her patience. Complaining to her spouse about her hard life had become a daily occurrence, and was an event from which he was more than eager to escape every few days.

Looking after 22 boys and more than twice that number of girls in the apprentice house was more than she could cope with sometimes. Washdays and suppertimes were often the most stressful, with so many of the apprentices falling asleep on their feet when they should have been helping her. Even on their day off, they showed no interest in play or leisurely pastimes, preferring to lounge about and sleep. Mr Sims had also noted that peculiar occupation among the apprentices and reported it to Dr Holland on several occasions.

The doctor had replied, "There is no disease of my experience, Mr Sims, which results in such tardy behaviour. Though, 'tis well known that the children of the lower classes do tend to bouts of lethargy and contrariness."

Peter Holland was the personal physician to the Greg family and his employment also as a factory doctor was singularly unusual. Samuel Greg felt that the health of his workers was important so that with medical care, a little nursing and recuperation, they could return to work all the sooner after any injury. Most other mills would simply replace injured workers as soon as possible.

It was not uncommon in mills everywhere for younger apprentices to be so weary that, while tending to weaving or spinning machines, they fell into the mechanism and suffered appalling injuries. When the number of factory inspections was stepped up later in the century, more and more reports would reflect such tragedies arising from the hazardous tasks that children were expected to undertake.

After a long day, Mrs Sims was looking forward, in the evening, to sharing the new bottle of sherry with her husband in their cosy lounge. He had taken delivery of it that morning when he had gone to the Old Bridge at Broadheath Warehouse to meet the barge from Liverpool. There were new stocks of raw cotton for the mill to be collected. Mr Sims did not mind filling-in occasionally for sick draymen, as it gave him the opportunity to grab the odd bargain at the back door of the warehouse. That day, it had been 'a bottle of the best Jerez' all the way from Spain. This had meant he had left the boys gardening at the apprentice house under the supervision of Jason, one of the older apprentices. Jason had failed to notice later that Thomas and Joseph lay hidden beneath one of the overgrown hedges between the garden and an adjacent field of barley. The other apprentice boys, including those who knew about the escapade, pleaded ignorance when questioned by Sims on Sunday morning. They were curious to see whether Thomas and Joseph would get away with it.

"One shilling and a few pence was all that Sefton collected, yesterday from his overtime pay. Priestley was due five pence and three farthings."

"Well, they're not going to get far on that are they, Mr Greg?"

Richard Sims was in the mill manager's office reporting the runaways to the mill owner, Samuel Greg. He'd explained how he felt that the fault in the matter lay with Mrs Sims and Jason.

Greg had put him right about where he felt the true responsibility lay and Sims' ears still rang with his master's reprimand.

"If you recall my words, Mr Sims, I said we must keep an eye on Joseph Sefton for a while when I refused him permission for some time off."

"Aye, that's right, Sir—to see his mother in Hackney, I heard. Watched him close, we did."

"Hmm, not close enough, I think. And you say you have questioned the other apprentices, Sims?"

"Oh yes, Sir. Gave 'em a right roasting, I did. Oh yes. But they claim to know nothing."

"And no beatings, mind; I won't have it said that the Gregs beat their apprentices, you know that."

"Course not, Mr Greg. Me and the missus are both good Christians like you and Mrs Greg."

It had slipped the superintendent's mind at that moment that he had, occasionally, applied his boot to the seat of the pants of not a few of the boys. Samuel Greg was confident that the two would not get very far before being apprehended. But this did not prevent him from expressing his displeasure with Sims. He waved a handful of papers at Sims.

"I can ill afford to lose two workers on whom I've spent money training up, when every day we're receiving new orders for yarn. Orders we need to meet if we are not to lose future custom… It's most inconvenient…"

The mill owner stood at the window for a moment, deep in thought, looking out across the cobbled courtyard at the recently completed extension buildings. His manager, chief clerk and the superintendent shuffled silently where they stood, each loathed to break into the ponderings of their stiff-backed, immaculately clothed employer.

"I'll get a message to the justices in Wilmslow and Congleton, Mr Sims. In fact, you can take it for me, when we finish here, I think. They won't get far before they're arrested for vagrancy. We know that they they're headed for London, so I'll send a letter to the Hackney workhouse committee, to warn them to expect visitors, just in case the stupid pair get that far before they die of exposure… Go get the horse and gig cart ready, Mr Sims."

Richard Sims nodded then glanced towards the clerks that sat in the adjacent office.

"Might need money for the toll gates, Sir?"

"Not for Wilmslow, Mr Sims. We're still talking about setting up the Trust, but yes, you will for Congleton."

Sims still seemed reluctant to leave the office, pausing at the door, the turnpike fee still in his hand.

"What is it, Man? You need to hurry if we are to catch them."

"Pardon me for saying so, Mr Greg, but today's me one day off. So, perhaps I should tell one of the stable lads to get it ready, eh."

Mr Greg fixed his superintendent with a one-eyed look that made the large man's knees shake. Greg's left crescent eyebrow floated above such a stiletto stare that Sims felt a piercing prickle in the back of his skull. The rumble from Greg's throat exploded his words once more, like a slap across Sims' sideburned ruddy cheeks.

"You are lucky to still have a job, Man! Get to it now before I throw you and Mrs Sims, both, out on your ears. Get out!"

***

"What you doing down there on your knees, Tommy?"

"I'm praying, Joe. Asking The Lord for his guidance on our journey to London…" He closed his eyes again and muttered some words of repentance.

"You ain't in church, Tommy. You're under that there old oak tree. It probably don't count, Pal."

"I know that, Joe, but it don't seem right, somehow—it being Sunday and all. We'd a' been to church twice by now. This morning… And then again for evensong afore the sun sets… Don't seem right not to pray."

"Well, I reckon we've only got a couple more hours of daylight, Tommy, and no sight of Congleton, yet. So, if you've finished resting on your knees for Jesus… Maybe we can sing a couple o' hymns on the road, eh?"

Joseph's enormous grin betrayed the fact that he was making fun of Thomas, who replied, "I don't care what you say, Mate, it makes me feel better if I think God's looking out for us. 'Sides,

I promised Mrs Bawtry I'd say me prayers and she said God will still be looking down from the sky, from heaven."

"Say one for me, Tommy, and let's be off, eh? I don't suppose a bit of religion is going to hurt us. But we might find we're saying our prayers in jail if we get picked up as a pair of vagabonds. Come on, Pal!"

They had been walking for another two hours, chewing on concrete crusts of bread and bruised apples donated by Mrs Bawtry, following a path through Brereton forest when Joseph stopped suddenly.

"I need a pee," he said, running to stand behind a tree. "See if you can find where that river is, Tommy. We're out of water."

Thomas listened to the sounds of rushing water from the River Dane and headed deeper into the woods. The chill from the shadows seemed to grip him and pull him away from the remains of the June sunshine that flickered through the leafy canopy. An overpowering weariness was telling him to rest but he dutifully pressed on towards the sound and now the smell of the river. He sat down and looked down the slope beneath him, smiling at the water that glimmered through the trees.

"Found it," he said, throwing his sack down and closing his eyes, with his back resting against a giant oak. Tiredness was slowly winning after three hours hiking almost without a long stop. The shadows of the trees in the gathering gloom caused moments of fear to creep down Tommy's spine but he had to rest—just for a few minutes. He knew that Joseph had been correct in telling him that they would need to move off the road when they lay down to sleep, hiding from any interested 'nosey parkers or trouble makers'. *Surely, this would do,* he thought, *better give Joe a shout.*

"I've found the river, Joe! I'm over here by—"

It was at this point that Thomas' drooping and heavy eyelids snapped open. It was at this point that he became aware of an enormous furry brown head, with a big black leathery nose that sniffed the sack beneath his feet. At this point, Thomas' throat refused to make a sound, soprano or baritone, or any tone, try as he might, nothing came out of his mouth. The fear that paralysed the muscles controlling his voice had spread to the rest of his body, and all that the young boy could do was stare into the big brown eyes of a big brown bear.

"It's most inconvenient, Hannah. Too much trouble, just when we need to expand the mill. Business is good, very good, with all of the new orders that seem to be arriving almost daily."

"Yes, Samuel," replied his wife.

"We need to install another water wheel for the new machines I intend to order… We can't afford to spend money on apprentices, only then to have them run off to London."

"You said that they wish to see their mothers, my dear?"

"It's just not a good time, Hannah. Poor excuses for some days off that's what it is, I'll be bound. Ah, here's Peter now. He'll tell you the same… Good evening, Peter and how is Mrs Ewart? Recovering from her confinement, God willing."

Mr and Mrs Greg were returning home from the evening service at the Unitarian church in Wilmslow. Meeting Peter Ewart, his partner and chief engineer at Quarry Bank Mill, was fortunate as he could add to the reasons behind Greg's decision to not allow time off to apprentices. He suspected, accurately, that Hannah's arguments about the matter would be filling much of his time when they arrived home. Most immediately, she was much more interested in the health of Mrs Ewart and the new baby girl, but had cause to chastise her husband about his next remark.

"Never mind, Peter, maybe it'll be a boy next time, eh?"

He was eager to bring up the subject of the new water wheel and so it seemed was the engineer.

"Now then, how long before the faithful River Bollin gets the new wheel to play with? Can we still run a few of the processing sheds while it's fitted?"

"Yes, I think so, Samuel. We'll take out that old 'un and replace it with the 20 horse-power unlinked to the main drive shaft. So then, we can link the two together and re-connect to the main shaft and be delivering triple the power of the original wheel—enough for the new bank of Crompton's spinning mules."

"That's excellent. Can't have machines and workers idle for too long and, of course, we'll be needing more workers too. I'm going to write to the parishes of Biddulph and Newcastle-under-Lyme to seek out more children from their workhouses. I've given up on the Wilmslow poorhouse for now—too many sickly and weak individuals if you ask me,

Peter… Doctor Holland tells me it will take too long to build them up, and that's time we haven't got, eh?"

Ewart nodded in agreement, while Hannah shook her head, saying nothing, saving her opinions about the matter for their evening supper.

The Greg's many children sat quietly around the meal table listening to their parents' discussion. Forming their own opinions was something they could not help doing, with the boys sure of a later position in the business, and the older girls often helping their mother in educating the paupers living in the apprentice house. But they too knew it would be a mistake to offer an opinion to Samuel until they were much older.

"Sims tried to pass on the blame to his wife and to Jason, who was in charge of the lads gardening yesterday."

"Jason is a bright young man who will probably do well with his figures and letters," said Mrs Greg.

"Hmm, yes, I agree with you, my dear. Probably become an overseer or maybe a clerk one day. But not trained up well enough by Sims to supervise a group of workers, if he can lose a couple of runaways just like that."

He snapped his fingers and the youngest boy tried to copy his father, laughing. Thomas, the Greg's eldest son, helped him in low, muttered tones under indulgent glances from their parents.

"Of course, he questioned the other apprentices about the matter, but, not surprisingly, could get nothing from them. I told him I hold him responsible. He's gone with messages from me to Wilmslow and Congleton and should return soon. At least, I told him to be back here before midnight. And tomorrow, I will write to get more children from the workhouses, we have room for almost a hundred now."

Hannah waited until Samuel had his mouth full of the beautifully cooked beef and was occupied with chewing it. She said, "Samuel, my dear, I don't recall what was so urgent to Thomas and Joseph that made them ask for more time off work. You said that they wished to visit their mothers in Hackney—but why now? I thought Thomas was recovered. Why go now when you need all the workers that you can get?"

38

Eleven-year-old Robert looked up with interest. He and his elder brother, of thirteen, were home for the holidays from their Unitarian school in Bristol. They knew that their father had begun his own training in the textiles business at the age of eight and later was in charge of some parts of his Uncle Hyde's linen trade, when only a few years older, still in his teens. Robert Hyde Greg, unlike the senior brother, would later follow his father into the cotton business, becoming a major figure in it and in the political world. Thomas Tylston Greg had little of Samuel's or Robert Hyde's business acumen and was destined to find a career in the Law or marine insurance.

"As you know, Priestley lost a finger and he claimed it still ailed him. Joseph Sefton has been suffering from a bowel… erm, a stomach complaint—not fit subjects for the dinner table, I think, Hannah."

"Of course not, my dear, but, as loving parents ourselves, we can understand children needing their mothers at stressful and painful times, surely? And, if we are to act in a truly Christian way, as befits our position, then, Samuel, I pray they will not suffer harsh punishment when they return?"

All of the children's eyes turned to look at their father and he resisted any kind of angry outburst in front of them. Samuel Greg felt that he knew the textile business inside and out, and that he knew how to manage people at all levels. He also resented any kind of interference from others when it came to running his own business—except, that is, when the advice came from Hannah. She had been responsible for many ideas about providing accommodation and education for his workers, especially the apprentices. She would later provide the finance for a school in Styal village and her suggestions, including the Unitarian chapel there, had all proven to be sound and even good business in some respects.

He remained silent for a few seconds, then nodded in her direction and then, smiling, quietly said, "You are right, Hannah. I promise you they will be treated kindly."

***

Thomas took in a long breath and let it out as a long, lingering sigh, waiting for the slightest smidgeon of courage to enter his veins. He waited for the bear to grab his foot in his mouth or in one of the clawed paws that were as big as Tommy's head. Slowly, he withdrew the foot nearest the bear and wondered whether he could get to his feet and run before he fainted away, or before the animal noticed.

"Keep dead still, Tommy," hissed a voice from behind his oak tree. It was Joseph. "I reckon he can smell them boiled taters in your bag, or an apple maybe?"

Close to tears, Thomas whispered back, "I've got no apples left, Joe. Must be Mrs Bawtry's taters. If I could reach my hand in… But I can't move or—"

The bear lifted a paw and started to drag the sack from beneath Thomas' other foot when Plonk! An apple landed right in front of the bear's nose, only to instantly disappear into his mouth. Swift as it was, it gave the boys ample opportunity to catch sight of two rows of terrifyingly large canine teeth. Holy day of the week it may still have been, but that view of so many sharp teeth gave the God-fearing Thomas cause to blaspheme between his own gritted dentition, "Jesus Christ! I'm going to die, Joe."

Plonk! Plonk! Plonk! Boiled potatoes from Joseph's sack began to gently rain down from behind the tree and land near the bear's head to be quickly eaten. And then the last one rolled back to settle beside the boy's thigh.

"Oh no," groaned Thomas and, while he summoned up the nerve to flick the potato closer to the bear's head, the furry face stretched closer and closer towards his groin. But the bear seemed to be held back from reaching past his knee. Hot breath flew out of the black leathery nose into Thomas' face, ruffling his hair and making him feel much closer to fainting away.

"He's tethered, Tommy," whispered Joseph. "Look at his back leg and his neck. There's a metal collar or something attached to a chain. Must be tethered to a tree, I reckon. That's why he can't quite reach the tater. Flick it to him; he's not going to eat you while there's other grub around, Pal."

The two boys jumped with shock when a rasping man's voice came out of the dense bushes behind the bear.

"Eh up, Fella, you're right there tha knowst. Old Atlas is a might partial to boiled taters. I thank you for sharing your grub wi' him while I was off down by the river, doing me business."

The bear had backed off to nuzzle the man's coat and a sack he was carrying. Now that the bear stood on his hind legs, they could see he was one or two feet taller than the full-grown man. Clumps of fur were missing from parts of the bear's body and hidden in the patches were his many battle scars. The man was tall and thin with an unruly red beard and walked with a stoop. His broken-toothed smile started at his eyes and seemed to be a permanent fixture.

"Here you are, Mate," said the man, tipping out a pile of mixed fruits of the forest—acorns, chestnuts and various berries.

"He can have some more taters," said a trembling, piping voice. Swallowing, drily, Tommy grabbed his sack and threw three more potatoes from it towards Atlas who swallowed them quickly and then returned to the few acorns left on the ground.

"That's mighty hospitable of you, young sir. I'm Jacob Bransby—Bransby the bear-man they calls me. We're here for the Bear Festival in Congleton that starts tomorrow."

He could see from the boys' expressions that they had not heard of it.

"There's going to be stalls with food and games; and cock-fighting and bear-baiting, and all sorts. That's how I make my money, see. Men bring their bull-terriers and put 'em to fight wi' Atlas. You can get as many as six of their best dogs in the same pit wi' Atlas and they bets on the results. Don't know why, cus Atlas always wins and I cleans up wi' me winnings. We come every year—don't we, Atlas?'

Atlas ignored Bransby apart from glancing at the empty sack lying on the ground.

"Oh yes, Congleton's famous for it, bear-baiting, along wi' a couple more towns we visit."

Unknown to Bransby, his particular brand of festival entertainment would be made illegal within twenty years.

Joseph and Thomas kept their distance from the bear but had gradually become braver and stood together watching him finish off the remains of the food.

"Hello, looks like we've got company," said Bransby, pointing back towards the road.

"Oh no! It's Richard Sims," exclaimed Joseph, jumping quickly behind the big oak tree to join Thomas, who hid there trembling even more.

"Don't tell him we're here," pleaded Thomas. "Please, Jacob. Don't tell him."

"It's all right, lads. Anyone who's a friend to Atlas is my pal for life. I'll see if I can get rid of him."

Richard Sims had spent just a little too long in a nearby tavern sampling the local ale, and was now in a hurry to get to Congleton. He was worried that he might not have enough money left to pay at the toll gate. In his haste to relieve himself at the roadside, he had not noticed the three deeper into the forest.

"All right, Mate, you here for the festival tomorrow?" asked Bransby as he drew closer to Sims.

"No time for festivals, Pal," snapped Sims. "Business to do there." He was feeling tetchy, knowing he would arrive back at Styal late, probably to Greg's displeasure.

"Bad day then? I was just asking like."

Ignoring the pleasantries of meeting with a stranger, Sims demanded, "Have you seen a couple o' lads on the road? A big 'un and a little 'un—skinny and scruffy pair they are."

"No, Mate, just me and me bear, Atlas."

Thinking that Jacob was being evasive, Richard Sims demanded again, "Stop wasting my time, will you? I just want to know if you've seen 'em—two skinny lads!"

"And I told you—just me and Atlas. Give us a roar, Atlas!" he yelled into the woods.

There was an almighty, "ROOAARR!" from the eight-foot-tall bear who had moved to the limits of his chains, and three people from Quarry Bank Mill nearly swooned on the spot.

"I'll fetch him over to meet you if you like," said Bransby. But Mr Sims did not reply because he was too busy running back to the road, tripping through brambles and ivy, scrambling over fallen tree trunks. Once he had calmed the horse down, Mr Sims, aboard the gig, was racing down the hill to Beartown.

"Right," said Bransby, "It don't look like he's staying for supper, so if you two gentlemen would like to get a small fire going, I'll nip down to the river and see if we've got us a couple o' fish to go with the rabbit stew in my pack."

The apprentices looked apprehensively at Atlas who had lain down on some fallen leaves and seemed to be gently snoring.

"Oh, don't you worry about him. That was just his little party trick that I taught him a few years back. He won't wake up now till he smells the cooking and I might have a fish for him, as well. I left four lines in the river. Usually, it's perch and tench along this stretch."

Later, Joseph and Thomas lay looking up at the stars trying to sleep against the background duet of snoring from Jacob and Atlas. They had decided not to go into Congleton, fearing that Sims would see them and that he'd alerted local authorities who would be looking out for them. Jacob had told them of a route to Kidsgrove that would take them around the town, where they could join up with a proposed new towpath for a big canal that was planned.

"Head for Harecastle," he had said before falling asleep.

"What do you reckon, Joe?" whispered Tommy. He waited for an answer but all he got was another gentle snore to form a trio of punctuated wheezes.

A34

N

0   2   4
Miles

Manchester *

Manchester Ship Canal

Stockport *

Broadheath
Warehouse

Quarry Bank
Mill: Styal *

Bridgewater Canal

Wilmslow *

Canal

* Alderley Edge

* Macclesfield

Congleton *

Sandbach *

Harecastle
Tunnel
Canal

Kidsgrove

Burslem
*

* Hanley

* Etruria

* Stoke-on-Trent

A34

Chapter 3
Legging Through Harecastle

"I don't reckon I can do this for much longer, Mister. I'm right jiggered."

Tommy's legs felt like lead. They were now so numb with pain from the effort of stepping along the tunnel wall that they had ceased to belong to him. Joseph was not faring much better even though he was bigger and stronger. The two boys had been grateful for the offer of a lift on the canal barge after walking for half a day to the outskirts of Kidsgrove. Charlie, the bargee, had told them they'd have to pay for the lift by helping him move the barge and over a hot drink and a large lump of lardy-cake, it had seemed like an easy choice. They thought that floating over the water with a full stomach and rested limbs, heading southwards, would be better than staggering along the dusty cattle road, thirsty and hungry for hours. Little did they know that lying on your back 'walking the wall' for hours would turn out to be just as taxing on their leg muscles.

"Yes, Charlie, I reckon we can do that, don't you, Tommy?"

"Yes, Joe," replied Tommy, slightly apprehensive but excited. "I've never been on a boat, Mister."

He didn't like to use the burly old man's first name out of an ingrained respect. And besides, there was something very scary about Charlie Capper that caused Tommy to keep his distance. Brindley tunnel ran for just over half a mile and later, its parallel twin, called the Telford also after its engineer, would make up the Harecastle canal tunnel. There was not enough width for a horse tow path and so, by lying on his back with boots firmly planted against the dripping walls, the bargee had to 'walk' his vessel through. It was hard work and over the years, Charlie had got the difficult journey down to a little less than three hours.

The occasional passenger was very welcome as it gave him the chance to entertain and be entertained, while smoking his pipe.

His amusement today was listening to the grunts and groans of the apprentices struggling to move the laden barge out of the Brindley as quickly as they could. He reckoned at the rate they were going, it would be nearly four hours, try as he might to gain more speed by uttering words of encouragement. Tommy's skinny frame had given up on him and Joe was close behind.

Charlie decided to continue with his story. "Aye, when yer in 'ere and it's a rainin' and a stormin' overhead thar never knows which end o' tunnel the Kickrew Boggart gunner be screamin', see."

He often found the tale of the Kidsgrove ghost, or boggart, encouraged the slower passengers to put in more effort once they were deep into Brindley's tunnel. The local legend about the murder of a woman by her husband had been embroidered in many ways. Charlie preferred the version about hacking the poor victim's head off with the sharp edge of a roofing slate before throwing the corpse into the deep dark canal water of the tunnel. The incentive to move their legs a mite faster had been found.

"She screams all the more, see, lads. 'Cause ont' night she was murdered, there was a fearful crashing and a thundering from the storm. We're comin' to the spot where body were found just now, see. Shall I hold me lantern up so's you can see the spot?"

"No, no, yer all right as you are, Charlie. I could wish ye hadn't told me that," wheezed Joe and moved his aching legs faster, clogs slipping and sliding across the mossy wall. Tommy had his eyes shut tight, squeezing tears of dread out of the corners, and he held his hands over his ears. The ghost of a woman's torso floating by with her head bobbing alongside it, screaming at him was an image he could do without. Somehow, without any prompting from Tommy, his legs had suddenly gained more strength and speed so that the barge began to move imperceptibly quicker. Charlie Capper's fruity chuckles echoed from the tunnel walls and even Tommy's pressing palms could not keep them from his ears.

***

"Just another couple o' miles with the 'orse haulin' the barge, lads, so yer welcome to stay on it till we unload at Kidsgrove."

Even though Joseph would have liked to lead Charlie's horse, Jasper, along the tow path, he lay lifeless next to Tommy, each waiting for feeling to return to their lower limbs. Jasper had been re-harnessed to the barge by Russell, the bargee's younger business partner.

"That's very kind of you, Charlie," said Joseph, still gasping for air.

Thomas said nothing clearly but his moans were meant to show gratitude like his companion. The pair were so physically and mentally exhausted, they were barely conscious.

Charlie smiled and added, "Aye, there'll be a wagon waitin' there for to take some o' this lot to the coal mines, see."

'This lot' consisted of dozens of roughly-hewn pit props and felled trunks of timber from Macclesfield Forest, as well as many boxes of silk from the mills of Congleton, Stockport and Macclesfield. The return journey's cargo would be coal supplies for the hearths of those same towns. More often, there would also be crates of cheap pottery destined for the shops and market stalls found along the high streets of the northern towns.

Kidsgrove was a rapidly growing town since the expansion of its coal mines and would continue to grow for a few more decades with the increasing demands from the various steam engines now in so many industries across the country.

Russell, who had led the horse over the top of the tunnel, stared at the boys and whispered, "What d'yer reckon then? Looks like we got ourselves a couple o' runaways, Uncle Charlie."

The business partnership made a curious pair. When working, Russell had to call Charlie the 'gaffer' and he was a large bald man with an enormous white beard, while his nephew was a wiry young man not much bigger than Tommy. The few wispy whiskers around Russell's chin and cheeks could have been shaved away by a few licks from a tomcat's tongue according to Charlie.

That morning, his sister-in-law, Hetty, had insisted that her son and the gaffer wore the new uniform she had made for them when they were working. "Believe me, Charlie," she had said as she waved them goodbye, "it will lend you an impression of respectability when looking for more business. You mark my words."

So, they wore their new worsted waistcoats and neckerchiefs with pride. The red shoddy-silk neckerchiefs had matching handkerchiefs hanging from the breast pocket of their waistcoat. Unfortunately, these became rather oily and grubby after a few hours on the canal and undoubtedly would attract some words of criticism when the men later returned to their home in Hurdsfield near the town centre.

It was a short walk from there to Brocklehurst's 'thrown-silk' mill where she worked at a spinning machine. Macclesfield had another mill on Chester Road that also was water-driven but the war between France and Britain had caused such a demand for silk products, particularly silk buttons, that steam power would soon replace the water wheels. Macclesfield's boom in silk weaving was to mirror that of so many cotton towns around northern England. Manchester's expansion into the cotton trade, over just a few more decades, would mean it later earned the name 'Cottonopolis' as the world centre for textile manufacture.

Hetty was an overseer of a throstle spinner producing the cheaper short silk from recovered silk waste. Although it had an inferior lustre, it was often blended with softer spun silk.

The hard travails of the child apprentices that Hetty daily supervised pulled at her heart strings and caused her to vow that Russell would never become indentured to a textile mill. He had served his seven years apprenticeship with his father and uncle and knew that he would be taking over the business, eventually. His contribution to the work had been essential during the last four years after his father had been drowned. Rusty Capper had slipped into the canal trying to prevent a load of timber falling in and had become trapped under the murky water by the weight of the logs floating above him.

The boy silk-throwers, as they were called, had to run some 22 yards, backwards and forwards with the yarn, twisting it to make a finer, stronger thread. This meant running up to 14 miles every day, often barefoot. Like Tommy and Joseph in the cotton mill, the boys' jobs would often include piecing, or joining, broken yarns with their bare hands so that the important business of manufacturing fine thread was not slowed or stopped—despite sore and blistered palms.

Hetty had managed to purchase a small yardage of crimson short silk for the men's new 'uniforms', as she was pleased to call them. As a dedicated supporter and regular attender of the Macclesfield Sunday School, Hetty had a keen interest in the welfare and education of children. But unknown to her, this saintly activity would be used by her husband's brother and her son for their own wicked intentions with regard to Thomas and Joseph.

Russell had a keen instinct for 'making a few extra bob' whenever he could, especially if it entailed not using too much of his limited muscle power. About a year earlier, he and Charlie had been rewarded with a few pounds from the local justices, when they had disclosed the whereabouts of an apprentice who'd intended running away to join the navy. It was not uncommon in recent times for young men to suddenly find it was their patriotic duty to defend 'Good King George' against the French and 'that murderin' tyrant, Boney'. The unfortunate young man concerned also desired to escape from his unpleasant tasks in a tanner's yard and, while sleeping off his 'wall-walk' through Brindley's tunnel, was easily apprehended by the local constables. Russell was keen to gain, perhaps, twice as much reward by giving up Thomas and Joseph—he had a plan worked out.

Charlie Capper was well aware that his nephew had inherited his brother's brains and felt confident that Russell would improve his business somehow. But Charlie had sufficient 'nous' to keep a sharp eye on Russell to make sure he stayed on the right side of the law. He hadn't objected to making money out of the absentee leatherworker by doing his duty as an honest citizen, so listened carefully to Russell's scheme as they walked the towpath together. They glanced across at the two boys lying prone on top of the packing cases, visitors to the land of Nod.

"See, Uncle, if you keeps 'em busy, I can run on ahead and get constables or t' Beadle. What d'yer think?"

"An' what if they won't come, Russell? Thee art gunner look reet foolish, eh!"

"They believed me last time so I reckon there's a reet good chance they will agen... Any road up, I'll come back wi' some bread an' cheese for lunch or summat, see."

"I suppose I could persuade 'em to tek a job in silk mill wi' Hetty or mebbees on t' barge wi' thee an' me?" mused Charlie.

Feeling that he had to humour his uncle, Russell replied with some enthusiasm, "That's a right good scheme there, Gaffer. Here tek this. It's some of me last week's wages that I ain't spent yet. Tempt the two on 'em wi' that."

He gave Charlie a half-crown who thought for a few seconds and added, with slitted eyes on the shiny coin, "Aye, and I've got another in me pocket. Should get the pair on 'em pondering a while on what ter do, I reckon… Hmm, it could work."

"Of course, it will, Gaffer. If they teks the money we'll still make a tidy profit on a few quid reward money, eh?"

"Right, Russell, you be on yer way quick, afore they come to. Leave the rest to me!"

***

The late afternoon sun was behind a few strands of clouds and Jasper had his chestnut nose into a bag of oats while Joe stroked the horse's lean flank. He was strongly of the opinion that Charlie and Russell did not care for their horse as strongly as farmer Parbold and would have welcomed the opportunity to take over Jasper's welfare. He knew that it would never happen but hoped that one day, his fortunes would change for the better and he would work with horses somehow. Sitting under the shade of a large willow tree, Tommy was giving Charlie's words some consideration.

"I recognised them callouses across yer palms see, lads. Apprentices what our Hetty looks after 'as got same hands, see. It's from piecin' broken yarn on a spinner, ain't it?"

Neither boy replied, finding something interesting in the canal to stare at. Piecing involved the action of rubbing the palms of young hands together many times a day, week in and week out. Rubbing the cotton or flax fibres held there produced frictional heat and that assisted the re-joining of broken threads. Sadly that heat also produced blisters and soreness across their palms and the resulting scaly callouses tended to cancel out the softer palmistry lines of health and fate. Fateful tangents of calloused skin pushed ever closer towards the children's struggling lifelines that marked out their destinies.

"She teks good care on her apprentices. Gives 'em a good edication in t' Sunday school. There's a good few gooin' up ladder, tha knowst. Getting' ter be owerseers an' such... Clerks even—'sgood money an yer sits darn most o' day! Aye, reet good jobs then, tha knowst."

Joseph thought it was time to interrupt and change the conversation, slightly.

"No, Charlie, if I come back this way, I'd rather work with animals—especially horses, like old Jasper here. Maybe stay on a farm..."

"Spinning and doffing's all right if you keep your hands out o' machine," added Thomas without thinking, nursing his injured hand. Doffing the mule involved removing full spindles of yarn and replacing them with empty ones, ready to receive the spewed out yards and yards more thread from the ever active machine. This was while under pressure from the mule's overseer, the adult who was paid as a pieceworker. Kicks and cuffs from this charge-hand would not be rare and often unseen by 'blind eyes' when increased production was the rule of the day.

The pain was now considerably less and he remembered Mrs Bawtry with fondness. Both boys had private moments of sadness, conversations of pathetic consolation together, when they each realised that they could not recall their own mother's face to memory. Lost in this for a few seconds, Tommy had to be shocked back to his present predicament—his friend obliged.

"You could feed the chickens, Tommy! You'd like that! And collecting the eggs every day. What d'yer think, Pal?"

"Eh! What! What chickens, Joe? Have you lost yer mind?"

"On me farm when we come back this way, Mate!"

His ruse brought his friend out of his despondent thoughts and Joseph asked Charlie a question to push things further along, well away from the subject of textile mills.

"How long has Russell been gone? Does he always go on ahead like this, Charlie? You seem a bit short-handed to me." The gaffer was not fooled at all by the change of subject. He was absolutely certain now that the two were apprentices running from a cotton mill. But his expression betrayed none of his thoughts as he drew out from his pocket the two half-crowns.

"Well, you are correct there, young Joseph. I could do wi' a couple more fellers very soon, see. If you were to stay wi' me an' help us unload at Kidsgrove, there's one o' these each for yer."

Two shillings and sixpence, half-a-crown, was more than either could receive as wage earners in weeks at Greg's mill. But as paupers from the poorhouse, they were entitled to nothing more than their keep. Their eyes grew big and round at the thought of how useful it would be on their continued journey to London.

"In fact, boys, on the way back come an' see me in Macc for a job, permanent like. As I says, I'm expectin' ter get a new contract with the openin' o' this new section o' the Trent and Mersey cut, see… Ee, I can remember when it were called the Grand Trunk. He's a clever feller that Brindley, tha knowst—brought me a bit o' business over t' years…"

While Charlie mused on the past for a minute, Joseph came to sit with him and Thomas, and Jasper turned his attention from a bucket of water to some wild flowers growing under the willow.

"Cause they'll be bringing up the chiny clay from Cornwall, see… For the potters in Stoke and Tunstall and them, see. Well, I can bring it down wi' me silk an' such like. Yer'd get more than a half-crown every week. Here—"

Charlie flicked a coin to each boy who caught them and felt the welcome heaviness in their palm, lost in thought.

"Tell yer what, fellers, keep the money till we've unloaded this lot in Kidsgrove. You probably earned most of it movin' t' barge thro' Brindley's any road. And yer might decide to stay wi' me for a few more weeks. What d'yer think?"

Neither boy replied. They glanced at each other and stared again at the canal avoiding Charlie's penetrating look. The few seconds, in which Tommy felt an uncomfortable sense of guilt as temptation grew inside him, became unbearably long.

They each looked around at their surroundings, anywhere but at the bargee.

"Who's that with Russell?" shouted Joseph, suddenly.

He was looking down the towpath in the direction of their destination. When Charlie looked in the direction of Joseph's pointing finger, he saw two large men carrying staffs of authority in their hand. His nephew was running alongside them. Their shouts were indistinct due to their distance from the resting trio. Gaffer waved to the approaching group and turned to say some words of comfort and encouragement. On the tow path behind him lay a coin glinting in the fading sunshine. But the boys had gone.

***

"I think... We'd better... Find a different road... Into Stoke... Don't you, Pal?"

There was no reply from Thomas. For the second time that day, he was too exhausted to say much. The pair had fled as fast as their aching legs could take them into the nearby woods and then collapsed into an enormous stretch of scrub and bracken. Joseph listened to his heart thumping in his chest then his attention was caught by a skylark singing high above them. Try as he might, he could not hear voices, or the rustling of thigh high grasses, or runners of bramble scratching and snatching at the breeches of their pursuers. There was just the sound of his companion's breathless wheezing, in between sobs of despair.

"It's all right, Tommy, Lad. I think we've lost 'em. You just lie there awhile. Get yer breath back... I'll take a peek and see if it's all clear... Maybe I can find some friendly farmer, like old Parbold... Get us summat to eat and drink."

He began to rise up slowly from his crouching position. "Don't leave me, Joe!" pleaded Tommy. He was terrified and felt almost completely beaten by their circumstances. And without the older boy near him, he felt that he had nothing left, no nourishment, no money, no hope for the future and no will to continue. He feared he would die in that lonely spot under the ferns. "What are we to do, Joe? It's hopeless," he whimpered and blubbed himself into a frenzy of tears and drool. Joe patted his friend's back and sat down beside him once more.

"Don't you worry none, my mate. I ain't about to leave you. No, no, Pal. There's nothing gunner tek me away from me best friend... You rest now and then we'll go and look together—find some grub and a drop o' tea. You just see."

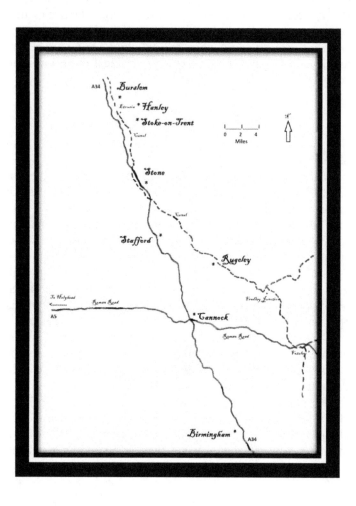

Chapter 4
Burslem Bottle Kilns

Mrs Brightwell wet her fingers and snuffed out the cheap smoky candle beside her husband's sick bed. She dared not touch him in his troubled sleep, he was finally resting from his awful injuries. Abe Brightwell was a good worker in one of the potbanks built on the Sandbach road in Burslem, the same road that further along held rows of cheap terraced cottages, one of which was where the couple lived with their three children.

She pursed her lips in contemplation and slowly shook her head, whispering softly to herself, "You silly man. I towd you and towd you never to break down the clammins too soon… Now luke where weem at… Tish! Maisters care nowt for thee when orders are pilin' oop." *And they'll care even less when yer not fit for work,* she thought, softly closing the door behind her.

Abe had been one of the gang of saggar makers, ordered by the factory owner, to collect the fireclay boxes from the bisque oven a day early. Usually, two days were allowed for the stacks of clay wares to cool after firing in a bottle kiln but the owner was anxious to send the order out quickly. When the kiln was opened too soon, the inner walls were still red from the intense heat and so the men covered their faces and hands with wet rags. They also wore three or four layers of coats and trousers for protection. The vertical stacks of saggars, called bungs, were so tall that the men used ladders to collect them. Abe had fallen from his ladder and broken an ankle as well as scorched the skin from his face and hands when he'd landed badly.

The Tuesday sun had not quite set but Sarah Brightwell had needed the extra light from the candle to see the swollen skin in the gathering gloom. A layer of runny butter carefully smeared over Abe's wounds did not seem to have improved things very much as Sarah could see 'water' gathering under the enormous blisters on his brow and whiskery cheeks. It was very unlikely in Sarah's opinion that he would return to work for a week or two.

She had lost two children, boys, to tuberculosis early in their marriage but Ellie, the girl that had survived, was now one of several young women employed as painters in the factory. This was one of the three largest pottery companies in the area, known for production of bone china. Ellie had inherited her mother's pretty face and auburn hair, though Sarah's was peppered with early grey streaks. The trim young woman was not paid as much as her father and her wages may well become the main source of income for the family if Abe was to be laid off for a while.

Ellie's two younger brothers were also employed in a potbank, as helpers to a pot-thrower, one turning the wheel and the other preparing the clay and 'carrying away'. Like their dad, the boys each had jet black hair but most of the time it appeared to be greying from the clouds of dry clay dust in their place of work. All of the youngsters there looked permanently pasty-faced due to that dust which everyone also had to breathe in. It was very hard work for which they rarely brought home more than a shilling to eighteen pence after a sixty hour week.

Joshua and 'little' Abraham were paid directly from the wages of the potter and often had to wait for their money. This was because he was paid in gold and had to change it every week by visiting a local public house. Their 'maister' was often unsteady on his feet when counting out the few pennies into his apprentices' hands after a bout of drinking too much ale. Abe and Sarah had concerns about the two boys waiting there for their pay. They were both under ten years old and sometimes returned home from the pub, much too late, of a Friday evening smelling of beer and tobacco. It was the same story for many of the children tied to doing menial work for the very many pot-throwers and plate-pressers around the Potteries.

Apart from Ellie, none of the Brightwell family could read or write much more than their own name, there being no time for education, this despite repeated offers from the local Temperance Society and the Sunday school where she taught, occasionally. When not working, the children wanted to sleep most of the time, too weary to think of childish play.

Three hours later when the youngest children were in bed, asleep, and Ellie was finishing up some sewing for her mother, Sarah was in their back-yard checking the clothes on her washing line. Her experienced hands were running over the few items hanging there for dampness and their readiness for ironing. It was far too dark to see them clearly and the light from the tallow candle balanced on top of the mangle was just enough to prevent her stumbling. With her arms full of clean clothes, Sarah stopped as she turned to enter the back door, her heart racing, as she listened. There was whispering coming from the privy just a few feet away.

"Who's there? What are you about in my yard?" Then she shouted, "Ellie, come out here, will you? And bring that brass poker with ye!"

Sarah stepped inside the scullery and dropped the clothes into a wicker basket. Grabbing the poker from her daughter, whose eyes were fearfully wide, Sarah banged it against the mangle, making a terrible clanging sound. No longer as slim as her daughter, the buxom mother was ready to split a few skulls if she had to. Ellie tried to look brave and held the yard broom for a weapon in her right hand. The other held the candle aloft, its flame spitting and sputtering with the shaking of her limbs.

"Come out now and be off out o' here afore me husband comes down. Ah'm tellin' thee, he don't tek kindly to burglars! Come on! Out! Now!"

The squeaky privy door slowly swung open and two teenaged boys slowly stepped out looking sheepish and dishevelled. Their faces were grubby and small twigs, leaves and seeds clung to their matted and muddy brown hair.

"It's all right, Missus, we ain't burglars nor footpads nor nothin'," said Joseph. "We just hid in there for the night. We'll be on us way now."

"I... I... Just need... To—"

Then Thomas fainted and fell to the ground. Ellie screamed in surprise. Joseph stared at Mrs Brightwell with fear and a plea for help in his eyes. He knew that he had not enough strength left in his body to carry Tommy away and was close to tears. She instinctively recognised his plight, and dropped the poker saying, "Ellie, grab his feet, will you? Me and his brother will take an arm each."

There was a pause when Joe and Ellie looked at each other, unsure about the wisdom of the woman. Reminded for an instant of her two lost sons, who'd have been of similar ages to the apprentices in the sorry state before her, she took their brown eyes and snub noses to be evidence of siblings.

"Come on, the pair of ye," she ordered. "Into the parlour with him—the poor duck. Luke at him. He's wastin' away to nothin'. Can't ye see?"

* * *

"So, yer not brothers then."

"No, Missus, but we are best pals and we're on our way to London. Tommy's lost a finger and wants to see his mother and with a bit of luck, I'm going to see my ma, as well."

"Well," said Sarah fixing Joseph with a knowing look, "yer not from these parts. I can tell a Manchester voice when I hears it."

He opened his mouth in protest but stayed silent when she raised a hand and added, "Don't get chattin' now. Get some o' that food darn yer first."

It was early the next morning and Mrs Brightwell, having attended to her husband and the three children, was trying to 'sort out the lodgers' who had slept on the rag rugs overnight in her parlour. The three young pottery workers had to be in their workplace for six o'clock and had been stepping around the sleeping strangers for nearly thirty minutes before they left the house. Both lodgers had kept their eyes shut, pretending to sleep during the whispered but rushed breakfasts of bread and tea-kettle broth. They felt too embarrassed to engage anyone in conversation. No one was fooled by the pretence at all, each recognising flickering eyelids from personal experience when resisting the morning call from parents.

As soon as the Brightwell children were gone, their mother was noisily setting the table with two bowls of watery milk and oatmeal ready to rouse the boys. She had tapped the table sharply with a spoon.

"Get thesen washed and comb some o' that countryside out o' yer hair, you two lads. Then you can tek a bit o' breakfast with me."

Despite her brusque attitude towards the pair, Sarah had decided to help them and on the previous evening, while Thomas and Joseph slept, she had taken some time to persuade Abe, who was naturally concerned for her safety.

"Nay, Abraham, they're just two runaways from somethin' or other. I'm going to see 'em safe on their way and that's that. The young 'un needs feedin' oop. Just a scrap of a boy he is. 'Tis only Christian thing to do."

"Well, thee be careful, Sarah. Ah can still get downstairs ter see to 'em if they cause trouble—one leg or nowt!"

"Dunner thee fret thysell, Abe. Just you stay there an' get better, me duck."

She faced the boys across the table and smiled to see a bit of colour returning to their cheeks and watched them tucking in to the simple meal. They smiled back, heads full of questions but afraid to speak much in case it invited too many queries from this kind woman. Sarah had a lot to say and was so tempted to take the pair under her wing, so much did they bring to mind her own deceased boys.

"Drink oop that tea while it's still hot. There'll still be a drop more in pot after I pour some for me man."

They guzzled the tea down and politely paused while their teacups were filled again. Sarah left them for a few minutes while she took Abe's tea up to him.

"Missus has been right kind to us, Joe," said Thomas.

"Aye, she has that, Tommy."

"Do you reckon we've given the constables the slip now?"

"Reckon so, Pal. But weem still got to be careful what we says like."

"I can still smell smoke, tha knowst. What with all them chimneys, I suppose." Sarah's heels could be heard clomping down the uncarpeted stairs.

"Hush now, Tommy. Here's the missus."

Still smiling, Mrs Brightwell re-entered the parlour and said, "Now luke at you two. A reet bonny pair o' young men I'll be bound. A bit o' decent food inside o' thee and a rested night can always work wonders, I think. Might be a bit o' lobby come dinner time, boys." Seeing the frowns on the boys' faces she explained, "Like a bit o' stewed meat and vegetables from us garden, tha knowst."

"Like lobscouse," said Tommy. Occasionally, lobscouse was a treat for the ninety occupants of the Quarry Bank apprentice house and Tommy was about to say so when Joseph gave his ankle a gentle tap.

"That's real generous of you, Missus," said Joseph, smiling back.

"Ah think thee can call me Mrs Brightwell if ye like. And what are you called? Thee were so jiggered last night you just fell to sleep as soon as ye finished eating."

Before lying down to slumber before the dying embers of the parlour fire, they had enjoyed a relative feast in their short-lived experience. Mrs Brightwell had revived the senseless Thomas with a wet cloth and a bowl of cold water while Ellie warmed up a little pease-soup and divided the remains of a small mutton and onion pudding between two plates. Her mother had steamed it earlier in the day and after supper had kept the paltry amount back for her husband.

There was always very little food left in their pantry but Sarah could not bear to let children be in her house and go hungry. A slice of her sweet raisin cake, even though stale, dipped in the smallest amount of honey and tea brought moans of appreciation from the famished runaways just prior to their eyes closing for the next seven hours. The faint image of a wooden plaque bearing the faded words 'God Bless This House' lingered briefly behind their heavy eyelids. When they awoke, the plaque was still there on the mantelpiece and there was a damp and smoky aroma of brimstone pervading their nostrils to remind them of the bottle kiln forest surrounding the terraced cottages.

After telling her their names, Joseph asked about all the dozens of chimneys they could see from the backyard.

"We could hardly see where we were last night and it's still very smoky even by day."

"Well, you see, Joseph, that's all the bottle kilns that gives us all work and wages. Once the kilns are all fired oop, there's soo much smoke that at times ye can hardly see yer hand in front o' yer face."

"So, all them chimneys are from the pottery factories then?"

"That's reet, Thomas, only all us calls them potbanks, not factories."

"Like cotton mills instead of cotton factories?"

Joseph sighed and cleared his throat, signalling to Thomas not to say more, but it was not noticed—at least not by his travelling companion.

"Which mill are you two from?"

"Manchester," replied Thomas, proudly sticking to their story.

"I hear there's lots o' mills in Manchester?" She waited for more information but was disappointed. Joseph changed the subject once more.

"Something wrong with Mr Brightwell is there, Missus?"

"Aye, Joseph, he had a bad accident at work. Much like thee and your hand, Thomas. Must 'a' been very nasty to cost yer a finger, me duck. What were yer abart?"

"I was doffin one of the mules." Now, it was Sarah's turn to look confused. "I mean swoppin' over the full bobbins, like, doing a bit o' piecing… And I caught me finger in a spinner, one of the wheels."

She was none the wiser but her look changed to one of caring and sympathy, gently placing her hand on his cheek.

"Let me tek a luke at it, Duck. Ah can see a kind hand 'as wrapped it oop for thee but that cloth needs changin' or it'll be septic."

"Oh, you're all right, Mrs Brightwell. It's stopped hurting now. That's right ain't it, Tommy?"

Thomas said nothing, just glumly nodded. Although Joseph cared about his friend's welfare, he knew how fragile his emotions became whenever a woman showed him the kindness that his short life had lacked. It was then that Thomas became vulnerable to questions and too revealing about their journey's destination and the situation they had left behind.

"You've got enough on your own plate with three children and a sick husband to care for."

"Dunner fret thesen, Joseph, there's never enough love in this world. 'Appen God saves us some for the next, eh? We can but hope…"

She turned to Thomas who sat quietly weeping, tears streaming down his cheeks once more.

"Oh, me duck. Come here, Tommy lad." The mother in Sarah could bear it no more and she rose from her chair to embrace him, allow him to cry himself dry in her arms.

***

Try as he might, Joseph could not help but blush whenever his eyes met those of the pretty paintress, Ellie Brightwell. It was the same for the girl whose cheeks coloured each time he smiled at her and offered to help with her various housekeeping tasks: washing pots; sweeping the hearth; fetching coals for the fire. His handsome face and manly voice held an attraction she had not felt before; inwardly chastising herself in case he was a villain.

Ellie and her mother were preparing a 'few things' for the two cotton apprentices to take with them on their journey south. Mrs Brightwell had slipped out after dinner to the market and returned with some food and cheap clothes. In addition to this she had spoken to Ruth, a good friend of the family, whose husband owned a barge bound for Tamworth. When her friend's children had been sick and her husband away from home, Sarah had helped nurse them back to health. Now that Ruth was offering to help while Abe was off work, Sarah had asked for an extra favour. Matt had agreed to give her lodgers free passage if they would help load and unload along the way as well as tend to the canal locks when necessary. She had no doubt that they would jump at the chance to get so far along their journey, so had said yes on their behalf.

Spirits were high once again for the travellers, after they had been worried about losing so much time re-gaining their strength in the Brightwell's home. It had been four days since they had absconded from Quarry Bank Mill and they were not even half way to London according to Matt.

"Well, Tommy, Pal, it looks as though we're in luck again. Ellie was saying as how this man, Matt, is a good and trusted friend. She is sure that we will get a good way along if we lend a hand with his duties… Why hast thee got that silly grin on yer face?"

"I think you would believe anything that lass tells thee, Pal. You're a bit sweet on her, ain't ya?"

Joseph's mouth opened but no speech came out. Slowly, his newly tanned features became suffused with crimson. Tommy's grin grew wider and he nodded.

"I thought so… But I'm not frettin' about it none. Let's just get to it, eh? Get aboard that boat with this trusted friend. Ellie's word's good enough for me… It's a pity we can't do owt to help the missus an' her family, eh, Joe? Return the favour like."

The ability to communicate had returned to Joe and he murmured, "Yeah, you're right about that, Pal. But we've still gotter be careful what we say. I reckon constables round here are still on the lookout for us."

"Right, lads, Matt's waiting ont' front doorstep for thee. We've put some cheese and bread and a few taters, apples and turnips in yer sacks. And there's an extra water bottle full o' cold sweet tea. Keep ye going for a day or two. Now don't go eatin' it all at once. I know what growin' lads are like."

Sarah reached out to hug each boy in turn and a small family procession followed them out onto the street. The pink sky was assuming its more confident golden hue as the sun took hold of the day and dawned it behind the smoke of the bottle kilns. The bespectacled and moustachioed Matt was standing at the kerb, cap in hand, leather bag at his feet. Crowds of workers passed by behind him in both directions; mumbled greetings stumbled through wisps of smoke.

"Mornin' to thee! G'mornin'! Owdo!"

"Owreet!"

"Fair to middlin', thou knowst!"

"Mornin', Sarah, mornin', lads, art owreet? How's Abe?" Matt asked, taking hold of the handles of the bulging leather bag. Beneath the faded fabric of his old tweed coat was an obviously powerful frame that stood six feet tall in bare feet.

"Oh, he's bearin' oop, thank ye, Matt."

"Will ye be comin' back to see us, Tommy?" piped up little Abraham. The Brightwell brothers and Thomas had sat in the backyard for thirty minutes the night before, chatting and whittling as the sun set. Joseph had been busy scouring a couple of old saucepans, pointlessly trying to achieve a shine on them in order to impress their big sister.

"Dunno. Maybe," replied Tommy reaching into his pocket and taking out his shiny half crown. "Mrs Brightwell, I want you to have this. It'll pay for our food and board—and, and… Them new clothes you got us. You've been right kind to us all along—and you've got a sick husband off work. We won't never forget you… Will us, Joe?" He quickly wiped away an insistent tear with the back of his hand.

Joseph said nothing. He was so horrified that Thomas had kept the coin. It meant that Charlie and Russell Capper could claim that they had stolen money from the two bargees. What if the 'trusted Matt' knew Charlie? Had word reached Matt already and all this kindness was just a ruse to trap them? What would Tommy say next?

"Oh, no, me duck. It's been a pleasure to give thee a lift on yer way to see thy mother. Clothes were cheap from the hock shop an' I've never begrudged a bit o' food for hungry kiddies. Put yer money away, Lad. Ye gunner need it afore long, I'll be bound… But I'm touched by yer gesture, Tommy… You're a good lad an' thy ma should be proud o' thee." Sarah dabbed her eyes with her apron.

A long silent sigh of relief escaped from Joseph's lips and his ready smile returned. Only Ellie noticed and she gave him the smallest hint of a smile when she caught his eye again. But then Matt said, "C'mon, you two we'd best be off. Weem got a bit of a walk fust to Etruria where she's moored."

The two boys looked at him with frowns of puzzlement.

"Lady Ruth. It's what me barge is called. It's only abart a mile or so." Matt then fixed Thomas with a curious look of his own. "Where did ye get such a sum o' money, Lad? That's more 'un a week's pay for boys round 'ere."

Joseph held his breath again. What could he say to satisfy their listeners? Everyone's eyes were focussed on Thomas. He had to speak up quickly before Tommy spilled the beans.

"Oh," said Thomas, nonchalantly, "me mother sent me a crown a few weeks back; to help us on our journey like. That's what we've got left."

He had thought things through before slipping into his dreams the previous night. He hated lying to Mrs Brightwell, hoped that God would forgive him, but dared not tell the truth. Then he stood before Sarah and continued, "Will you just take the money for the clothes?"

"I tell thee, Child. It was just a few pence. No, no."

"Here, Mrs Brightwell, use it to buy some medicine or a treat for your sick husband," said Joseph suddenly, pressing a handful of pennies and a threepenny bit into Ellie's hand. She looked to her mother for advice but Joseph had turned away. He was desperate to get on with the next stage of their journey, even though he had a lump in his throat and knew he would miss the Brightwells, the pretty paintress in particular.

The three travellers shouldered their bags and sacks then set off through the bottle kiln forest, for Cobridge Road towards Etruria. When Matt turned to wave one last time, he grinned at someone who was at the bedroom window. Seeing this, Joseph and Thomas looked up to catch a challenging glare as the smile disappeared from the face of Mr Abe Brightwell. At least one person was glad to see the back of the boys from their cottage.

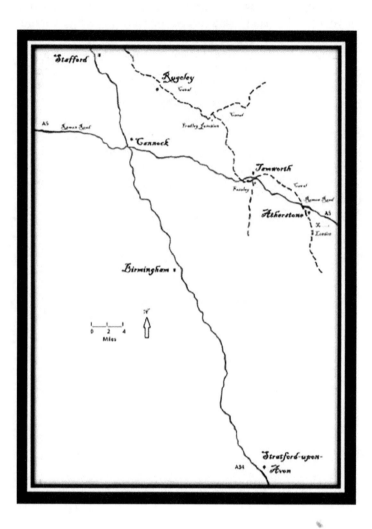

Chapter 5
Stone, Rugeley and Tamworth

Etruria was the centre for Wedgwood's famous pottery works and, as they helped Matt load some precious crates of Jasperware, the boys stared in wonder at the palatial building facing them across the Grand Trunk canal.

"Who lives there, Matt?"

"Why that's Etruria Hall, Josiah Wedgwood's little pile, Joe. Not bad, eh?"

"Does he have a big family—a lot of children like?" asked Thomas.

"I s'pect so, Son. I dunner know. To tell thee the truth, Tommy, I canner get bothered to know much abart the toffs… So long as they pays me reet, on the dot like, that'll do me."

Matt made sure the crates were tied down securely, wiped the black dust from his hands, after checking the load of coal already held aboard and said, "Reet, lads, you two get ont' barge and I'll lead the mule on. We'll stop after a couple o' hours for a bite."

Pausing briefly to admire the red and white prow of the narrow boat, where they assumed the words 'Lady Ruth' gleamed at them in the sunshine, the apprentices jumped aboard. Matt took hold of the mule's halter.

"Reet, walk on, Bob. Next stop, Stone."

It had come on to rain after forty minutes travel along the tow path and the boys had been encouraged by Matt to shelter in the cramped boatman's cabin. They were watching the world go by the tiny windows when the words of a song reached their ears. Thomas heard it first of all:

"…Along by the lock-side, And down by the dockside…"

"Listen, Joe, can you hear it? Matt's singing—listen…"

"…I drift down a slow path, My life is a tow-path…"

The boys smiled at each other as the poignant words floated along to the steady tread of the man and his mule. When he came to the end of the song, they went back on board and gave him a small round of applause.

"That were right cheerin', Matt," said Joseph. "Can ye teach us the words to your song?"

"Aye, appen I can later, eh."

"How come you've got a mule pulling the barge, Matt? Don't you like horses?" asked Joe.

"Oh, ah likes 'em well enough, Lad an' ah did have an 'orse when ah started int' haulage business, like… Must be twenty odd years back."

He gave his mule a friendly pat on the side of its neck, adjusted his cap as the two kept pace together and continued, "But me an' old Bob bin together for a few years now… Best decision I made, see.'

"But ain't horses stronger?"

"I had a couple more 'orses afore Bob but a feller tells me that mules is just as strong an' more willing to work longer for less food—cheaper to keep like."

"Oh, I see," replied Joe. "And was he right this feller?"

"Oh, aye, he were right. But it's not all abart cheapness is it, Bob?"

He took a carrot from his pocket and broke it in two to feed half to Bob. The mule nodded and plodded, chewing away.

"Ah tell thee, Bob here is cleverer 'an any 'orse I've had. He don't really need an 'alter tha knowst. Ah can leave him to pull for a mile or more wi'out me leadin' on, tha knowst."

"So, mules are cleverer than horses, are they?"

"Well, ah don't rightly know abart all on 'em, Joe. But this one is… An'…" He began to chuckle. "An' ah tell thee what, he don't mind me singin'… Do thee, Bob?"

The mule turned his head towards Matt and began snuffling and chuffing at his hand and pockets.

"See what ah mean. He ain't forgot t'other half o' that carrot. Hee, hee. 'Ere y'are, Bob."

"Can I walk with him a while, Matt?" asked Joseph.

"Course ye can, Lad. But don't be shocked if he gives yer a bit of a nip if he thinks yer ignorin' 'im."

"Ave you got another carrot?"

Matt chuckled again as Joe jumped to the towpath to swop places. He caught the carrot that was thrown to him and grinned at Matt.

"Dunner let 'im see it, Lad, or you'll get pestered to bits!"

It was late in the morning when they reached Stone where they took on another load. They had passed through a lock gate a few minutes earlier and it had not gone past Matt's notice that the two apprentices seemed to have an idea of what to do with the gates. As they passed through the fourth lock, the tail gates, which had finally lowered the water by nearly forty feet, Matt said, "You know, I reckon you two 'ave been on th' cut afore today. Now then, Sarah was tellin' me abart thee workin' in a Manchester cotton mill but you've bin bargin' afore. What dost think, Isaac?"

Isaac was the lock keeper who resided in a small cottage near to the tow path. He was already on his way back to the Star Inn to quench his thirst but made a quick reply over his left shoulder: "Aye, Matty, I reckon yer rart about that. See yer int' Star later." And he was gone.

The two apprentices looked at each other and Joe replied, "We got a lift for a short while, back aways. But I don't know where it were."

"An' I don't suppose ye know the name o' the barge man," said Matt, with a very knowing look and a nod of his head.

They shook their heads and he added, "Aye, well, it's not important to me so long as yer pull yer weight, then I'll be 'appy... Now then we've gotter get this coal to John Joule's Brewery up ahead, so after a bit o' snap an' a swift 'alf o' their best ale in Star we'll see to it."

The Star Inn was built at the side of the Trent and Mersey Canal, or Grand Trunk Canal as some sections were known originally, and was a major stopping point for stagecoaches between Holyhead and London. On this day, Matt and his two companions were sat outside the public house with a group of boatmen. In between finishing off their ginger cake snap and beer, they dredged up old tales and sang songs. There was a great commotion when the southbound stagecoach drew up and its passengers began to disembark. They were treated to a rendition of another bargee's song with Matt, Isaac and a few others in full throated voice.

"...Barges, I would like to go with you
I would like to sail the ocean blue
Barges, on the river you may roam
On the river, always, you're at home..."

A smart young man who descended from the coach was in a fine mood having recently stayed with some old Grammar School chums in Bury where he had been born eighteen years earlier. He was returning home, with William his brother, to Drayton Manor where his father was a powerful textile industrialist and parliamentarian. The Tamworth Member of Parliament had high hopes for all of his eleven children but especially for Robert, his eldest. The two young men, however, were not expecting to find a happy house when they reached Drayton Bassett village. Robert and his siblings had lost their mother and his father's second marriage was not working out well. Robert was looking forward to returning to Oxford University where he would later be awarded a double first degree in classics and mathematics.

Still full of joy from refreshing childhood memories and a successful hunt with friends, Robert and William paused to listen to the singers as they reached the final words of the song. Hoping to impress the two young women travellers standing nearby, Robert felt moved to compliment the manly choir:

"You have a fine voice and should be entertaining one and all throughout the land, Sir. Let me buy you and your comrades another fine ale to lubricate your tonsils before another ditty," he said to Matt, who tipped his cap respectfully.

"Thank you, Squire," replied Matt. "But I must be agoin' along see. We've got urgent business to attend to down that there canal."

"I am pleased to hear of such diligence, Sir, and would not delay any man from his employment."

The young man turned to Thomas, sat beside Matt, who had attempted to join in during the chorus.

"And you have a soprano voice, young sir, to rival any I have heard in my father's chapel or, indeed, any in Christ Church College, Oxford." To Matt he then said, "And is this fine fellow your son, for he inherits his father's strong singing voice. You must be proud."

Without a moment's hesitation Matt said, "No, Squire, Tommy and Joe here are alarnin' the business o' bargin'— apprentices like. An' we better be goin' on if weem going to finish afore the sun goes darn."

Thomas blushed, understanding little and saying nothing. Robert and William each took a small coin from their pocket dropped them in Thomas' lap and went towards the inn, Robert saying, "Well, I'm sure we wish you well on your journey, gentlemen. God speed."

Pausing briefly at the entrance, to allow the ladies to enter first, the two young men began to hum the tune that had entertained them. The sound of delicate laughter from the maidens was abruptly cut off as the stout door slammed shut behind them.

"I don't accept charity from anyone," growled Matt. "And I don't sing for us supper, for pennies or even silver. I sings for the pleasure it gives me."

"Thee has got too many principles, Matty," observed Isaac. "I wouldna' minded a free drink under the sun."

Thomas stared at the two sixpenny coins in his hand and muttered, "So, do you think I shouldn't have accepted the money, Matt?"

"Nay, Lad. Thee needs it on your long journey. Dunner fret thesen. It's just me an' my thoughts o' them as more privileged than us simple folk. See, the trouble wi' the gentry is they thinks they'm the only ones with a bit o' pride... But they're very wrong in that, an' one day... One day, all us 'simple' folks are gunner get together an' tell 'em some home truths."

"But they ain't all bad, Matt. Mr Greg's missus shows us a kindness from time to time and she nursed Tommy when his finger got cut off."

Joseph looked to Matt for a reply as they walked back to the Lady Ruth. He seemed to be ignoring Joseph, concentrating on waving his farewells to the other boatmen. But Joseph felt his opinion ought to count for something now that he was almost an adult.

"Look at that admiral that got killed savin' all of England in that Trafalgar place..."

Matt stopped walking, curious to hear the rest of Joseph's speech. "You're talkin' abart Nelson I reckon, Joe."

"Aye, that's 'im... Nelson, Admiral Nelson. Jason back at the mill read us a bit out o' the newspaper. He got killed last year savin' the country from Boney, that Frenchie."

"But he didn't do it all by 'imself, Joe. There was hundreds an' hundreds of soldiers an' sailors got killed as well. An' we're still at war wi' Napoleon, Lad. If it suited the gentry to call you two lads vagabonds, or paupers, or whatever suited 'em, then what do think would happen?"

"What d'you mean?" said Tommy.

"Why, lad, they'd put thee in prison an' then pressgang thee into the navy or th' army and send ye off to war. To get killed servin' yer country..."

The trio were stood alongside the barge. The two apprentices stared at Matt, eager to hear more.

"I've heard tell o' fellers agoin' home from the taverns near to docks, like in Liverpool, an' getting' their skulls bashed in by a pressgang... Then they delivers 'em, all trussed up like a chicken for the pot, straight on to the next ship bound for battle wi' the Frenchies."

"But," said Joe, anxiously, "they wouldn't do that to us, Matt. We know nowt about ships or shootin' guns."

Matt laughed and continued, "That dunner matter, Lad. Not when the generals an' the admirals need more men, or boys to fight. The laws are all on the side o' the gentry, the rich.

"Oh it'll 'ave to change an' only fellers like thee an' me are gunner change things, if ye ask me."

Thomas and Joseph stood thinking about Matt's words but he broke the small silence with, "Come on let's get on to the brewery. An' Bob could do wi' a feed. Come on."

***

The Lady Ruth made good time for the rest of Thursday pausing only at Ridgeley (Rugeley) to unload one of the crates of Jasperware from the Wedgwood factory. Matt was very concerned by two matters: that they unloaded the correct crate, the one bound for the Levett family of Milford Hall, and that the wagon sent to collect it was already waiting there. This meant there was a good chance he would reach Fradley Junction at Alrewas before dark to connect from the Grand Trunk Canal to the Coventry Canal and so proceed to Tamworth.

"Worst thing we could do, lads, would be to unload the wrong crate. See, this 'un says Milford Hall but t'other says Drayton Manor. Best thing my missus ever did for me business was teach me letters. Couldna' read a thing afore an' I got cheated an' all sorts wi' me contracts an' what 'ave thee."

"We get some schoolin' after work from Mrs Greg, but with overtime being demanded most every night, it ain't enough. I'd like to learn reading," said Joe.

"An' writin'," added Tommy.

"I noticed thee said the newspapers had to be read to thee. Tek my advice, boys, an' get theesells a good woman an' larn to read an' write if tha wants to get on. I tell thee true."

"Oh, you mean like Ellie Brightwell," said Thomas, grinning and poking his elbow into Joseph's ribs.

"Shurrup, Tommy," said Joseph, his ruddy cheeks burning.

"Aye, I noticed thee had a shine on Ellie, Joe. Ye could do a lot worse than that lovely maid, Mate."

"How did you get to marry your missus, Matt?"

"She used to come on short trips wi' me sometimes, Tommy, local 'auls like. Int' Potteries."

The boys tried not to grin at each other but their eyes gave them away and Matt saw them.

"Oh, I tell thee, no hanky-panky, like. She's like Sarah, reg'lar churchgoer an' got the right ideas about how to behave. Told me straight if we got spliced—"

"Spliced?"

"Married, Tommy. If we got married—if we were to marry an' 'ave kiddies, then no way was she goin' to bring 'em up in this 'ere little cabin. So, I larnt readin', with her ateachin' me, an' business grew, so we got a little cottage near to her best friend, Sarah."

The two runaways had warmed even more to Matt since he had taught them the words to a song and claimed they were his apprentices to the young men at the Star Inn. The elder brother, Robert, was to have another effect on their lives in the very near future, one much more serious than the cost of a few beers. In fact, Robert would be affecting many more lives within the next few decades. His opinions and decisions would resound down through the history of Britain and beyond its shores.

They arrived at Fradley Junction as the sun was setting and with five lock gates to negotiate, the lock keeper was unwilling to allow them through. He directed them to The Swan public house nearby if they needed refreshment or 'bed and board' but Matt was unwilling to part with the money.

"No, thee can go an' get some stew an' a drink if you've a mind. I'll pay for that an' then get yer 'eads down to sleep on them bunks int' cabin. Ah needs to see if there's a load to tek back wi' me on return journey. Can't afford to carry nowt on me barge see."

"We can pay some, can't we, Tommy?"

Thomas nodded and took out his few coins and the half-crown.

"Look, lads, best keep thy cash out o' sight if thee doesna' want yer skulls bashed. You'll be helpin' me a great deal if tha teks care o' Bob. Wi'out 'im we're reet jiggered."

The two boys nodded and Joseph said, "Oh, aye, right. Of course, we can do that, eh, Tommy?"

Before Thomas had responded with a second nod of his head Matt had added a shilling to his open palm and was striding off towards the very large warehouse standing adjacent to the lock keeper's cottage. He had to find more business for his return to Stoke-on-Trent.

Under a beautiful blue sky and warming sun, the next day, Matt was feeling much happier with the world. He had arranged for a new contract in the Fradley Junction warehouse. He would be transporting two large consignments back to the Potteries which another bargee had failed to collect on time. One was a load of iron workings, meant for a Kidsgrove coal mine, while the other was a load of Ridgeley glassware, which a new department store was urgently awaiting in the fast-growing fashionable town of Hanley. When he had returned to the barge to sleep on the floor of the cabin the previous night, the boys were still awake and had told him more of their story, knowing they could trust him.

Matt had grown quite fond of the two apprentices over the two days, noting how caring they had been towards Sarah and her family. He was impressed by how keen they were to learn new skills and apply themselves with much enthusiasm and effort. Feeling concern for how they would continue the second half of their journey south, he tried to give them some advice, hoping not to offend. He could see how much Joseph wanted to appear confident and in command of things. In truth, Joseph's confidence had been intermittently battered by the events that had befallen them since leaving Styal. His belief in himself had see-sawed as regularly as Thomas' emotions had risen and fallen.

Having had barely five hours sleep, the three had eaten bread and butter as they got ready to negotiate the lock gates. Joe then settled Bob to his harness. Matt was anxious to check they were ready for the days ahead without him.

"Now then, when we get to Tamworth an' the two on ye part company wi' me don't forget what ah keeps tellin' thee. Stick to three things…" He waited, adjusting his spectacles on his nose, but neither of the boys responded. "Well, what are they?"

"Oh, erm…" replied Joseph, rubbing the sleep from his eyes. It was not yet six and the sun was struggling to rise through the clouds. He chanted the short list: "Stick to the hedges and trees if we see anyone who looks important ont' road; and… And stick to our stories about where we got money from; and erm, tell the truth about coming from Quarry Bank Mill but we got lost… 'Cause, 'cause… That can be checked an' they'll likely go easy on us if we do get caught."

"I'm not sure about that bit, Matt. About sayin' where we come from, like," said Thomas.

"It's only a bit o' my advice that ah think meks sense, Son. Thee doesna' have to tek it. Ah just knows if thee arrives in court an' ye lie an' yer found out—well, it goes much 'arder for thee. Ah've seen it 'appen to one or two mates o' mine, see."

The two young men looked at Matt and they could see the concern in his eyes. Suddenly, they believed that his advice came not just from his experience but from his heart. Suddenly, they saw another adult who cared about them and cared about what might happen to them in the future. This time, it was not a woman who could behave towards them like a surrogate mother. It was a man   a man they much admired—a man who they were going to miss. Suddenly, both boys realised how much they had missed having a father all the previous years.

It was with heavy hearts and many tears that they each hugged Matt nearly two hours later when the crate of Jasperware for Drayton Manor was unloaded. Matt had paid a drayman of his acquaintance to give the boys a lift on the Watling Street route to Atherstone, the same road that eventually would take them to London. The driver had scoffed when they asked when they would reach Canoc, telling them that Canoc was back the way they had come.

"Oh, no, thee left that many miles back. If ye stick to this 'ere road for a day or two ye'll come to London reet enough, oh yes, that thee will."

***

The Baronet, of Drayton Manor in the County of Stafford and of Bury in the County Palatine of Lancaster, stood at the window of his breakfast room watching his eldest son climb into the saddle of Charger, his favourite horse. Susanna, his new wife of less than a year, came and stood by him, linking her slender arm with his.

"Where did you say Robert was going so early this morning, my dear? It seems such a pity for him to be off out and about already with William and him arriving home only yesterday."

"He said he'd missed Charger and wanted to give him some exercise. I've sent two men down to Fazeley Junction to collect that crate of Wedgwood we ordered and Robert thought he'd ride to meet them."

"Oh, I see. He seems such a restless young man does Robert—so keen to make his mark."

"Well, Susanna, it is nothing less than I would have hoped for him—William and Edmund too, if I can have any say in the matter. There's much reform work to be done when I get back to The House and no doubt much of it will still require the attention of my sons in the future, God willing."

Robert, his brothers and his sisters greatly missed their mother, Ellen, and still felt uncomfortable in the presence of Susanna. Before Robert, who had the same name as the Baronet, had departed he had been discussing politics with his father. One of the last topics that had come up was the problem of runaway apprentices which had been increasing in recent years. While the

Baronet was of the definite opinion, like the mill owner and fellow reformer, Robert Owen, that improving working conditions would greatly reduce such absenteeism, both father and son agreed that many more servants of the law, such as police constables were needed everywhere.

Sir Robert had long been involved in the textile industry and like many others, joined partnerships to raise the capital required to set up spinning mills. Using Richard Arkwright's water frames, located by rivers and streams, he had set up a mill and housing for their workers at Burrs near Bury. Here, as at Quarry Bank, the shortage of labour in the local area was mitigated by employing pauper children as apprentices.

They were often imported from any parish that wanted them off their hands and were housed in a hostel of sorts, much like the apprentice house where Thomas and Joseph had lived for years.

The Tamworth MP had introduced the Health and Morals of Apprentices Act that attempted to limit the number of hours that child apprentices worked in mills, obliging the owners to provide schooling of some kind. He was one of a few who were concerned by the working conditions for children in the cotton industry. Shocked to find that some of his own mills had been run by their overseers against his own more protective policies, Sir Robert later introduced a Bill which introduced even stricter limits on the hours all children could work in textile mills.

Robert had reached the London road and was allowing Charger to trot gently in the direction of Fazeley Junction when he saw a wagon in the distance coming towards him. He assumed it was the one sent by his father to collect the crate of Jasperware. When he imagined he'd recognised two of those aboard the wagon, he urged Charger to trot a little faster, and was surprised to see, not the two servants from Drayton Manor, but Thomas and Joseph. The song that they were singing was familiar to him but it broke off abruptly. Robert's surprise was infinitesimal compared to that of the apprentices.

The horses were halted and Robert said, "Hello, gentlemen. We meet again and still singing but no longer with the boatman."

The boys were so tempted to leap from the wagon and disappear into the surrounding forest but their legs, like their voices, seemed incapable of working. It occurred to Robert that they may have run away from Matt but his spirits were still positive and he had no desire to spoil his mood with unpleasantness.

"They're helpin' me collect some more goods—for return journey of th' barge, Squire. Weem off to Atherstone, like," replied the drayman.

He was not entirely convinced by the three rictus smiles he could see but Robert waved them on and wished them 'God speed' again. The apprentices resolved to dive into the hedges and woods immediately when they saw anyone on the road ahead during the rest of their travels, notwithstanding Matt's counsel.

The young man riding the fine stallion would become a member of parliament like his father before four more years had passed. When he succeeded his father, as the second Baronet, Sir Robert Peel would later twice become Prime Minister and Home Secretary, introducing prison and criminal-law reforms. His famous 'Peelers' would form the foundation of the Metropolitan Police force in 1829 and his government under Queen Victoria would most famously repeal the Corn Laws, a very popular measure with the working classes if not amongst his Tory followers.

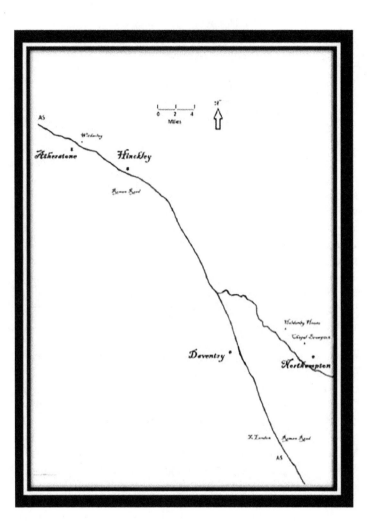

Chapter 6
Hosiery, Hats and Herding

Normally, Gabriel Chawker would pause from time to time, while at his woodworking, to glance down at the pile of shavings and sawdust gathering at his feet and reflect on things. The smell of the freshly cut wood would somehow bring on a philosophical mood to the moment and he'd find a reason to be at peace with his world—but not today. Replacing two backstick spindles in the back of a favourite Windsor chair involved sanding them down, staining them and finally giving them a lick of thinned shellac and were all skills he was proud of—but not today. His abilities to use a draw knife and spokeshave, when coping and shaping the spokes from an old cartwheel to repair a neighbour's kitchen chair, were well known. Normally, Gabriel would find the brief search for the right piece of wood, ash or elm, and his transformation of it into a piece of furniture, to be something satisfying, fulfilling—but not today. Today, Gabriel was angry about his own clumsiness at such a busy time on the farm. Anger had replaced feeling foolish and sorry for himself because shame was not going to get his cattle to market on time.

Standing on the arm of the chair, balancing there, while reaching for a taper and some tallow candles from the back of the top shelf of the dresser had not been a good idea. When everyone had rushed into the kitchen to find him lying, groaning, in the middle of a broken chair Gabriel had felt very foolish. Not only his rear end and back had been hurt, the fall had definitely bruised his pride. It had not helped when Martha had reminded him of the stepladder leaning against the wall beside the kitchen door, before turning to wipe away her tears.

"In too much of a hurry, as usual. I don't know, Gabriel, what if it had been one of th' children? Thee 'ad surely 'ad something' to say about it then, I'll be bound—tut! And did thee need to use that chair of all on 'em?"

The children had stared in wonder at their 'pa' for a few minutes, stifling giggles and grinning, then rushed back out to complete their chores around the farm. Chawker's farm, a Leicestershire small holding in the village of Witherley had not been doing well in recent years. With so many of his labourers leaving the area for better wages, in the nearby expanding towns of Atherstone and Hinckley, Gabriel was relying more and more on his family to help cope with the work. He was working all the hours he could and relying on his woodworking to provide a small contribution to the family's income, occasionally. But he was to be paid nothing more than some relief for his conscience when this repair was done. It was the chair in which Martha had spent many a late night and many hours of the day nursing their four children as babies.

There was a field to plough before winter frosts hardened the ground and apples and plums to pick, some ready for storage and some for sale on Hinckley market. He needed to take the fruit with him when herding his few cattle to the livestock market there. Gabriel doubted there would be time to collect the fruit. He had lost his two best workers to the towns and his family had become used to his muttered comments to himself: "Country larf foresaked for a felt 'at an' a pair o' cotton socks… Tut! What's next, ah says?"

The Hinckley hosiery industry had continued to develop and was paying wages of almost double that of a farm labourer. The war with the French had greatly increased the demand for officers' stockings, gloves and uniforms so that more and more textile workers of all kinds were needed in towns everywhere. The shortage of agricultural workers was causing much trouble to the farm owners.

As his cart reached the brow of an overlooking knoll the wagoner, a pinched, rat-faced, skin-and-bone of a man, turned to Joseph and said, "There y'are—Chawker's farm, just like ah tells thee."

The farm lay in the valley of the River Anker and the land was composed of a rich agricultural loam, unlike the land surrounding Quarry Bank Mill on the bank of the River Bollin, from whence the apprentices had come. Thomas and Joseph said nothing but took in the scene of hedges, orchard and vivid green pastures, smelling the mixture of cattle manure and fresh air. Breathing deeply usually resulted in a few catarrhal coughs from one or both of the boys, a symptom of cotton lung disease, common among mill workers and sure to kill many before their time. Cotton lung disease was also called brown lung disease or Monday fever. Medically known as byssinosis its symptoms were similar to those of asthma and the regular clouds of cotton fluff inhaled in a cotton mill caused the finer particles to irritate and clog the alveoli of the lungs. Stopping the early exposure to this dust would mean that most people need have no permanent damage, but the constant demand for mill work denied the less fortunate classes that freedom of choice.

Joseph spat into the roadside and replied, "And you reckon, Eric, that this'll be better for our travels than stoppin' in that hatting town back there."

The two were interested to see whether everyone wandered about Atherstone wearing a felt hat. In their isolated ignorance, living in Styal, they were quite unaware that the nation's centre of the hatting and silk trade, in Stockport, was just a few miles east of the Quarry Bank apprentice house. Despite his mean appearance, Eric Bates was a kind man. He knew something of the events that lay behind his passengers' trek, having heard it from Matt, and he had casually mentioned to them that 'if a person wanted to stay away from th' authorities it were best to reach Chawker's'.

Atherstone was a thriving centre for leatherworking, hats and cloth-making with much activity on that Friday, it being market day. Eric had earlier told them that the constables would be out looking for pickpockets and he knew of a farm where they could buy more bread and get fresh water away from curious eyes.

"You're sure the farmer won't just chase us away, Eric?" asked Thomas. He had flown for his life a few times from the owners of Styal orchards when he and his mill friends had been caught scrumping apples. When punished, it had cost them a few long overtime hours, collecting river cobbles, after mill working for nine hours. One penny an hour was all they'd received for that overtime in order to pay for the stolen fruit.

"Oh, aye, Gabriel's a good man. Known 'im for many a year, tha knowst… Good man owreet, oh, aye. He's had 'is share 'o bad luck 'o late as Chawker… But 'im an' 'is missus is salt o' th' Earth, tha knowst."

**

Three hours later, all three of the travellers aboard the wagon were close to the outskirts of Hinckley. Eric's wagon carried baskets of apples and plums, as well as the full sacks of the apprentices, and it led the cattle drive. Slightly fearful, Tommy and Joe each carried a willow switch stick and were bringing up the rear of the small herd of beef cattle. On their first arrival at the farm, Eric had explained their situation to the farmer and he was quick to turn it to the advantage of all—including Gabriel Chawker! A verbal 'contract' was made and sealed with a handshake.

He had decided that there was enough daylight left to reach Hinckley with his herd, it being only five miles further along the same drovers' road. Then, with some help from Thomas, Joseph, Eric and his eldest son, Henry, the herd would be penned in the livestock market ready for the auction on Saturday. The agreement was that they would all spend an hour collecting the fruit from his orchard, with Thomas and the youngest children gathering the windfalls separately for Martha to preserve and pickle later. Then, having loaded up Eric's cart, they had a brief rest and some food and drink, after which Gabriel gave the runaways brief instructions for herding cattle. It took them thirty minutes to get the hang of turning a young steer or heifer to the left or right and making it back up or move forward. They knew what to do all right but the problem was the animal—it refused to obey them most of the time! Twelve-year-old Henry found the timid antics of Tommy and Joe hilarious and kept repeating his own advice to them:

"No, no, thou must stand thy ground, lads. Th' animal feels safer in th' herd than on 'is tod… So ifn 'e sees thee as a threat ee'll run back to't, see!"

It did not help that after watching each attempt Henry found time to fall to the ground and roll around clutching his sides, so painful were they with the mirth he'd experienced.

Under a gloomy sky, a little after four o'clock, they finally set off with Gabriel allowing about ninety minutes for the journey. While explaining this, he noticed Tommy's missing finger and gave a few words of encouragement to him:

"We'll 'ave to get a move on, tha knowst. E'en so, ah canner see us reachin' Hinckley while six… Eh up, Lad, ah sees ye been careless wi' thy fingers lark me!'

The stocky farmer held up his right hand to display only two fingers and a much calloused thumb. When sharpening some his tools a few years previously, a scythe had slithered from the wall where it carelessly leaned and chopped off the two smallest fingers as he bent to pick up a sickle. The whetstone Gabriel wielded quickly became red with his blood and had stayed so stained ever since to serve him as a reminder.

"Took me a while lark, Tommy lad, but ah can still do me jobs around th' farm. E'en a bit o' woodwarekin' if ah've a mind… So, let's get to it, eh!"

Each of the boy's sacks contained as many apples and plums as they wanted to carry, together with one of Martha's freshly baked cobs and half a pound of Chawker's cheese. Things were looking good until they had covered hardly two miles on the road when the dark clouds that had been lingering on the horizon rushed to meet the cattle drive. The torrential summer shower was of the type that insisted on soaking them to the skin before they had time to find a hood or waterproof oilskins, neither of which the apprentices possessed in any case.

The rain had cleared up by the time they had penned the herd in Hinckley and, despite the soaking and the muddy manure splashed up to their thighs, both apprentices felt well satisfied with their day's achievements. Over the five or six days travelling their stamina had built up and they were enjoying the open-air life. They had agreed together that they would continue walking until it was too dark to see, counting on three more hours of daylight. Eric was returning to Chawker's farm to sleep in the barn, as arranged with Gabriel, while father and son had found a room for the night at the Tin Hat public house. When Gabriel told them of the tradition about drovers drinking a bucket-full of ale from the tin hat on top of the flag pole in the market place, the apprentices said that they would rather find a water pump to get clean. This they did and after all the farewells, they set off at a brisk pace, full sacks over their shoulders, determined to make it to Towcester before dark.

Unaware that Towcester was over thirty miles further on, their energy and enthusiasm to make more progress would dwindle to nothing after they had covered another ten miles. Wearily, they found a reasonably dry spot in the surrounding woods before sleep overcame them and they lay down, too tired to eat beforehand.

***

"Do you mean to call in and see Ellie on our way back, Joe? Matt said if you was of a mind, she'd be a good catch. She's very pretty."

Thomas reached out and carefully picked a small handful of ripe blackberries from the hedgerow, popped them into his mouth then sucked his purple fingers. The pair had been walking for nearly twelve miles, after breakfasting on plums and a hunk of bread just after dawn, and were near Daventry. They were intent on reaching London before another two days had passed them by. Thomas was worried that failing to praise the Lord in His house of worship twice in one week would have serious consequences later. Joseph, being less committed to God, had more concerns about being arrested as vagrants with no obvious employment and the 'theft' of money from Charlie Capper looming behind them. He had thought about Ellie a lot since they had left Hinckley behind, distracted occasionally by some of the sights along their way.

"Well," he replied gruffly, "If we get a chance on the way back, I thought I might call in an' say good-day to the missus. She's a good sort after all… Ooh!"

His arms gripped his belly and he doubled up for the third or fourth time since breakfast. Too much fruit and little else was having its effect on Joseph's digestive system, still delicate a week later. Ignoring this, Thomas picked up on his sport of teasing his friend about the younger Brightwell female.

"An' you might say something to Ellie I dare say, eh?—Eh up, Joe, where's thee off to now?"

"Off to do me business! Ooh, hell's teeth!"

Still gripping his lower abdomen, Joe was struggling to quickly disappear into some scrubland to squat behind a hedge. Thomas muttered, "Oh, I see," then wandered the fifteen metres or so across the muddy road to peer through gaps in the hedge on that side of the drovers' way. In the distance, he could see a large herd of fallow deer and watched them for a few minutes before his attention was focussed on some rabbits in the field.

"Hmm, wonder if we could get us a cony or two for supper?" he mused.

"Come on, Tommy, Pal, best get movin' again and off the roadway, eh?"

Joseph's pale face had joined his companions to watch the deer briefly and Thomas asked, "Reckon we could catch us a bit o' meat, Joe? Look at them rabbits."

"You're dreamin' ain't ye, Pal? What do we know about catchin' conies? And we ain't got time to—"

"Hey! What'r you two ruffians about?"

The sudden shout startled the pair and they prepared to run as fast as they could away from the large red-faced man who had suddenly emerged from the gate to their right. He appeared to be carrying a large gun. Gripping their sacks, the boys turned left to face their escape path only to find another red-faced man walking towards them.

"I think they'd better come wi' us, Walter. Don't ye think?" said the one without the gun, a broad Scots accent betraying his roots.

"Aye! I do right enough, Jeb. The maister, he don't care much for poachers. We better tek a gander at what ye took in them sacks."

Joseph's immediate response was to upend his sack and tip out the remaining fruit, bread and cheese and his spare breeches and shirt into the mud.

"You got no call to accuse us o' poachin', Sir. We're on us way to London and stopped for a rest an' a bit o' snap. That's all."

He nudged Thomas and added, "Go on, Tommy. Show 'em what's in yer sack. Same as me, see. A bit o' grub an' old clouts is all we both got. We ain't poachers, Sir."

Walter, the estate gamekeeper, poked the toe of his boot among their belongings but was still not convinced.

"Nothing to see, I'll give thee that. But I heard the young 'un here talking about cooking rabbits."

Thomas' heartbeat was skipping along twice as fast as usual but he forced a smile at Walter and said, "Oh, that's only cuz I'm feeling hungry, Sir. We haven't eaten much at all since we left Chawker's farm."

"Oh, aye," said Walter. "And what mischief 'ave thee been up to at this farm I've never heard of? Apinchin' fruit by the look on it, eh, Jeb?"

"It's the farm up at Witherley," said his companion nodding knowingly. Jebediah Buckby had been the property manager for the nearby Borough Hill estate for many years. "Farmer Chawker's place. I know them well. Used to come down to his lordship's Christmas parties for the workers, but not this last few years."

"We was helpin' 'im herd his cattle to Hinckley market," said Joseph. "That fruit was some o' our wages, see."

"An' I was only lookin' at them deer, wanderin' how you could herd 'em, Sir," Thomas added ruefully. "I di'n't mean no harm nor nothin'."

"Never mind that," snapped Walter. "If you're about to herd them deer that's called rustling. Ye can get hanged for that. How do we know ye didn't steal some o' that farmer's cattle, eh? I think this is all a pack o' lies, Jeb. They don't know this farmer at all… They got caught by us afore they took some of the pheasants or the rabbits." The gamekeeper was bringing his shotgun up to point it at Joseph, about to order them back to the gatehouse with him.

"Let's not be too hasty, Walter," said Jeb, who was much older than Walter and more experienced at dealing with people. He gently pushed the end of the gun barrel to point it down at the ground and addressed Thomas. "Tell me more about herding Chawker's cattle, Laddie."

Thomas' voice had started to break during the past week and his soprano singing pitch wobbled and broke, with emotion and fear, as much as from his burgeoning maturity. In spite of this, he was determined to tell his tale to these two large and intimidating men, in their tweeds, gaiters and deerstalkers.

"Well, Sir, Mr Chawker's lad showed me an' Joe here how to use a stick to make a cow go for'ard an' side to side. And… And… "

Thomas had to pause for a moment as his mind became very confused with the feeling of panic that suddenly gripped his stomach. Walter had heard enough.

"I told thee, Jeb. Pure fairy tales from the little rogue. Any child can come up wi' that scrap of a yarn!"

"But it's true, Master, I tells—"

Jeb held up his hand, as much to stop Joseph's protests as the derision of Walter. "No, no, let the laddie speak. He needs a bit o' time to gather his thoughts. Right, lladdie, now you carry on and we'll listen." There was patience in his tone and a hint of enough kindness to encourage Thomas to continue.

"Well, we learnt that if we tapped him on't shoulder, like, then us could make 'im move t'other road."

"Right, laddie, and would that be the cow's left or right shoulder?"

Now Thomas was in a real fix. He was always getting his left mixed up with his right, and his fellow apprentices in the mill were often joshing him about it. All the logic and reason that had reluctantly gathered in his brain went spinning wildly away from him.

"I, I, erm if we, I mean... Can I show you on Joseph, Master? Please, Sir, please let me. It'd be a might easier for me to show you, if Joseph was the cow."

Jebediah Buckby was now a grandfather with several grandchildren, including two of a similar age to Thomas, whose confusion he could understand. An amused smile played across the features he tried to keep looking stern. His companion snorted in disgust but said nothing. Jeb gave Joseph a nod to indicate it was acceptable for him to be 'a cow'.

With Joe bending forward at the waist, to bring his shoulder level with that of Thomas, his pal picked up a twig and flicked him with it on his right shoulder adding a shout of: "Ya! Hup there!"

Joseph obediently turned left and gave a sort of trotting performance away from the others. Thomas chased after him and tapped his left shoulder, adding with even more enthusiasm this time: "Ya! Ya! Hup! Hup! T'other way, cow! Come on there! Whatcher about, hey!"

Obediently once more, Joseph turned but this time to his right, growling an angry, "Easy on, Tommy," under his breath.

Neither man could resist smiling now at the unexpected afternoon amusement provided by Thomas Priestley. In equal measure, they found the embarrassed frown and disgusted look from Joseph towards his friend just as amusing.

"And is there anything else you would like to tell us about the farmer, Laddie? What is his name? And the name of his son, who you say showed you how to herd cattle?"

"Oh, it was Gabriel Chawker, Sir, and his son Henry showed us the herdin'. His missus gave us some fresh bread an' cheese and she was called… "

"Martha," interjected Joseph, as he paused from wiping mud from some of the apples on the road.

Then for extra measure, Thomas waved his injured hand at them and added, "And Gabriel has an 'and like mine, Sir. Only he has lost two of his fingers—not one like me, see."

"Hmm, that's right," Jeb was quite convinced now that the boys were not poachers at all and that they had been herding for Gabriel Chawker. Walter was pretty well convinced but wanted to have a say in things.

"How old is this son of the farmer? The man you called Henry, I think you said."

"Oh, he weren't a man yet, Master. He's a lad no older 'n meself, I'd o' thought. What dost reckon, Joe?"

Joseph had been busy putting back their scattered belongings into their sacks during some of the conversation.

"Aye, Sir, he'd be about twelve or thirteen like Tommy here." He ventured further, "So, now you know the truth on it can we be on us way, like? Only we got a bit of a way to go afore dark, see, Master."

"Just you wait while we discuss the matter," ordered Jeb, the stern look having returned to his face.

The two men walked a short distance from the others and Jeb said to Walter in low tones, "I think they're telling the truth. Gabriel does have a son, Henry, who I haven't seen for about four years, not since he was still in frocks and rompers, carding and combing cotton bolls for Martha to spin. He'd be about the age they say, Walter. We'll let them go, I think."

"Right you are, Jeb. You know more of the folks than me."

When they returned to the apprentices and told them that they were free to continue on their way, Joseph helpfully said,

"By the way, Sir, I was wondering whether t'other side o' road is still part o' the lordship's estate?"

"Yes, it is, right up to the Northampton road. Why, what's it to thee, Lad?" asked Walter.

'Well, I didn't like to say before but, when I was behind the hedge like, I saw two fellers leggin' it away from me, towards that road you just mentioned, see, Sir.'

The two men immediately crossed the road and pointing eastwards, Jeb asked, "That way you say?"

"Yes, Sir; there's a bit of a path through the woods an' they took it."

"That goes towards Chapel Brampton doesn't it, Jeb?"

"Yes, Walter, and then it comes out near to Holdenby House, on Sir Clifden's estate."

"If we move quick we might catch 'em up," said Walter.

"Well, even if we don't, we could tip the wink to their man… I forget his name now."

"Jonas, the keeper's called Jonas. I see him often in the stagecoach inn."

They quickly disappeared into the woods and the two apprentices continued their journey, walking smartly down the drover's road, chewing cheese and hunks of stale bread.

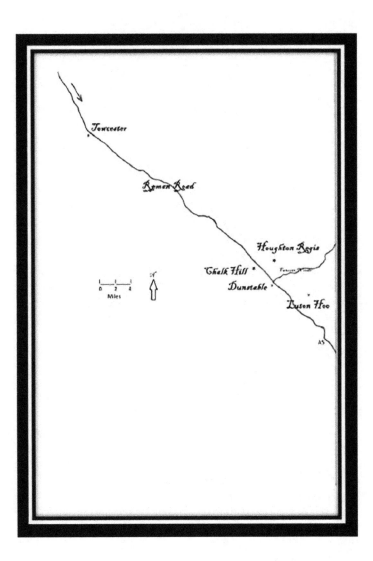

Towcester

Roman Road

Houghton Regis

Chalk Hill

Dunstable

Luton Hoo

0 2 4
Miles

A5

Chapter 7
The Downs and the Thomases

The apprentices made good time for the rest of that Saturday, leaving Daventry far behind and they would even hike past Towcester at long last. While covering the first mile, Joseph had insisted once again that they should keep a sharp eye out for anyone at all who was on the road ahead or behind them.

"We've got to stick to the woods and hedges, even lie in the ditch again if we see anybody, Tommy. That was another narrow escape back there with them gamekeepers. If either on us needs to relieve his self t'other, one keeps watch. All right, Pal—'as thee got it?"

"Oh, aye, Joe. Don't fret thesen… I wonder if they caught up wi' them two other fellers—them poachers."

"What two fellers would that be, Tommy?"

"Why them two poachers as took off when they saw you."

A big grin had spread across Joseph's face when he replied, "There never were two poachers, Mate. I made that bit o' tale up, tha knowst! I thought it would keep old Jeb an' his mate, Walter, a bit busy for a might longer, see. Give us chance to put a bit road twixt us an' them."

He slapped his friend on the back and added, "Just in case they should change their minds about us an' come back to take us pair o' nobodies to his high an' mighty lordship. A bit of a ruse tha might call it, eh?"

The pair now had to stop and surrender themselves to a few minutes of hearty laughter, slapping each other on the back and on the shoulder many more times, rolling about on the ground, holding their sides, breathless and merry. An interested observer might have noted that this display of merriment was in much the same fashion as that of their recent instructor in the art of herding cattle, one Henry Chawker, the eldest son of Gabriel. This same farmer who had seized the serendipitous arrival of Eric Bates and his two passengers to achieve the herding of his cattle to Hinckley livestock market; fortuitously giving those same two passengers a free pass out of trouble.

***

Coles Park in Hertfordshire was the country seat of Samuel Greg's elder brother, Thomas. It was located about 22 miles east of Dunstable which, unknown to the runaways, would be where they would arrive late on Sunday, the day after their encounter with Jebediah and Walter. By coincidence, on that same Sunday, Coles Park was the subject of a conversation between Samuel Greg and his eldest son, Thomas Tylston Greg. The conversation was taking place on their return from the Unitarian Chapel in nearby Cross Street. In Samuel's study at the family's Manchester residence, 35 King Street, father and son sat together beneath Greg's extensive collection of books and journals.

"Your mother and I have agreed, Thomas, that after you have graduated from Edinburgh it would be an opportune time for you to stay with your uncle at Coles Park."

Thomas was quite surprised at this news. Although he had rarely shown much interest in the business of spinning cotton, he had assumed that as the eldest son, he would eventually take over from his father, but it was obvious that he was in no hurry to learn much about it while in his teens. Samuel had an alternative in mind that was likely to appeal to Thomas and it had been discussed and agreed with Hannah and the boy's uncle.

"Yes, Father, and do you mean me to live there?" His father nodded.

"I see and why is that? What is to become of me there?"

"Well, as you know, your Uncle Thomas and Aunt Margaret have not been blessed with children these sixteen years and... with his many business interests, he wants to be sure that his financial affairs remain in the family. Aunt Margaret has an uncle on the Hibbert side of the family who settled in Kingston many years before you were born, and he has become a very rich and powerful man in the merchant shipping business. Aunt Margaret stands to inherit a great fortune and so is concerned,

93

with your uncle, that the family retains ownership and control of the various properties and trades in Kingston—in Jamaica."

Although he did not quite see how it would affect him at that moment, Thomas felt obliged under his father's piercing look to say, "Yes, I think I see. And I'm to live with Uncle Thomas when I have completed my education."

"My brother is well known for his welcoming nature, particularly to other members of the Greg family, and he and your aunt, Thomas, are very keen to have you stay with them as a son. You will learn much about the business of marine insurance and shipping."

The business of marine insurance and shipping did not especially have an appeal for the young man either but, on the several occasions that they had stayed at Coles Park, he had enjoyed the many times he had been invited to join his uncle at his sport. Uncle Thomas Greg was extremely keen on fox hunting and game shooting and seized every moment he could to be out riding across his Westmill and Knightshill lands. He had become the local squire and was spending more and more time there and less time at his business premises in London. Having adopted the Anglican Communion, he had become accepted into English society and frequently socialised with members of the medical fraternity and the clergy, including the rector at Westmill. This was in contrast to the stigma still attached to his family members and his many business associates, through their adherence to the Unitarian church. The label of 'Rational Dissenters' was still very firmly attached to those followers by critical observers, in private conversations if no longer so much in public.

Young Tom Tylston could think of nothing better than going to live with an uncle and aunt who would treat him as their own son. He imagined he could hunt, shoot and fish as much as he'd like, and riding with his uncle's pack of beagles was one of most thrilling experiences of his young life. He went to live with his uncle at Coles Park at the age of 15, where he stayed for another eight or nine years when he subsequently moved to the Albany, in Piccadilly, London. At this time, he was preparing to join the Greg's London partnership.

Thomas was unaware, as a very young man, of the sources of much of the wealth behind many of the senior members of the

Greg family, what became known generally as the triangular trade. In this, cloth and metal goods were shipped and traded to Africa for slaves, who were then sold to plantations in the West Indies; and then ships returned to Britain with highly profitable cargoes of sugar, molasses and rum. However, about three decades later, Uncle Thomas' nephew, Thomas Tylston, was to receive around £5000 from the Treasury in compensation for the loss of property and slaves in the Caribbean, after devastating storms there and the emancipation of slavery. The Hillsborough sugar plantation Thomas later inherited was in Dominica and its ownership would be signed to Samuel Greg, from his brother Thomas in 1819, in return for an annuity.

Tom Tylston would not prove to have the business qualities of either his uncle or his father and retired to manage the Coles estate at the age of 35. But like the senior Thomas, he became known for changing various farming practices, though his uncle was innovative in agricultural methods of ploughing and sowing. Unusually, Tom's mother, Hannah, who was known to have a kind word for anyone, was to comment that her son, when first at Coles, was not treated kindly by his uncle and this was due to his never having had children. This could be considered a somewhat harsh remark from anyone but particularly so from Mrs Greg, considering that her son arrived at Coles Park in the same year that Tom's aunt Margaret died. Her death probably contributed to his uncle's many low moods during the following decades.

The Greg's eldest son later left his father's study impatient for the next two years to pass. To become a favourite nephew, destined to inherit his uncle's fortune and live on an estate where hunting and shooting were favourite pastimes was more than he had previously considered possible.

***

Joseph and Thomas were taking a slow climb to the top of Chalk Hill, a disused medieval quarry, just off the Roman road. They wanted to see the sunset and get their bearings. It was on the north-eastern edge of the Chiltern Hills, known to the locals as the Downs. Having made their way back to the road, they'd passed by the village of Houghton Regis, collected some much needed fresh water from the brook, a small tributary of the River Lea, and now they waited for the sun to touch the horizon. This was on the recommendation of a charcoal burner, whose acquaintance they had made much earlier in the day, when coming upon his camp in Fancott Woods on the other side of the same Roman road. It had not been their intention to stray so far from the road but, when they had seen in the distance what looked like a large crowd of men and dogs approaching from Dunstable, they had no choice. When they had run about a mile into the woods and were very short of breath they rested, coughed, listened and smelt the wood smoke.

"What dost think, Tommy? Can you hear them?"

"No, Joe, I think they must've been after a criminal or something and passed by us further up the road, up the way we've come."

"Aye, reckon you're right, Pal. Wonder where that smoke's comin' from? Unless my nose is deceivin' me I can smell cooking."

Despite the rapid beating of their hearts, as much from panic as from running, the pair began, with a mutual nod of agreement, to follow their noses for the source of the cooking. Another hundred yards into the wood, they came upon a clearing of about sixty to seventy feet across with a muddy mound some twenty feet in diameter. The mound was six or seven feet high in the centre and as they went closer, they could see it was not just of mud but many sods of grass were interspersed amongst the soil. What amazed them most was the wispy grey smoke that escaped from the centre of the mound.

Cautiously, they approached further into the deserted area and with a resigned look Joe said, "This is where the smell came from, Tommy, but I can't understand how we thought it was something cooking."

Before Tommy could reply a deep voice, rasping like a spade scraping the wall of a deep well, made them jump.

"Vaire is summin' acookin', my friends. An' you're very welcome to join us if you've got summin' to add to the feast. Cuss I wasn' spectin' no guests, see."

They turned to their left to see the sootiest person they had ever seen who was not employed as a chimney sweep. With him was the sootiest looking lurcher they had ever seen. It was the breed of dog Tommy and Joe often saw catching rats around the mill's buildings. The man was very tall and thin with bony, soot-stained hands and arms that protruded from his long, soot-stained, fustian coat sleeves. On his feet were well-worn, blackened boots. It was his face that gave them most misgivings. Gaunt, like a corpse, with sunken cheeks and large staring eyes set into sooty looking sockets. He had no visible whiskers but his greying lank hair hung across his features and a prominent nose emerged from within, a dewdrop hanging from it.

The lurcher at the man's side had something of a brindled black and tan look beneath the soot, with rough, staring hair from nose to tail, and eyes to match his master's. The panting dog's many sharp teeth were visible and a low growl told them it was not pleased to see strangers.

"Hush, Charc, tha's no way to welcome guests," rumbled the man, an unfamiliar southern slant to his voice.

The dog looked up at the man and obediently sat when he extended a large bony hand to Joseph saying, "Sprig, I'm Sprig an' I must attend to me bacon in the pan over vaire afore it gets too fried an' crispy."

The smell of the bacon was so tempting to the hungry travellers that after shaking his bone-crushing fist they each followed him in a kind of daze, muttering:

"We might find a couple o' taters tha knowst."

"I think I've got an apple—an' a... Yes! A turnip!"

Thomas had plunged his hand to the bottom of his sack and retrieved a slightly shrivelled example of that staple root vegetable. He held it aloft triumphantly like a prized pot of gold—his shouts masking the complaints from his grumbling stomach. The mouths of both boys were watering at the sight, sound and smell before them, and their knees weakened with desire for a little taste of bacon.

On the other side of the smoking muddy mound there was a small fire with a large, blackened pot suspended over it. Crackling gently at the bottom in a pool of hot fat were three thick rashers. The tall man glanced in the pot, sniffed and the dew drop disappeared.

"Sit vee darn, friends. Less see what ye've got to offer us, eh... Hmm, well they're a bit muddy; but I reckon vat'll wipe orf, don't you?"

Sprig dropped the vegetables into another pot of water, took them out, wiped off the mud with a grubby cloth that had been hanging over a washing line between two saplings and then he peeled the vegetables and the apple with a very sharp clasp knife he'd taken from a deep pocket. With hardlya glance at his hands, he began slicing each offering and dropping the slices into the pot, which immediately objected to the addition by producing violent hisses and pops for a short time before resuming its gentle crackles.

"Cam, sit vee darn. Charc won't hurt vee—lessen I tells 'im to. Hee, hee, hee! Now stop it, Charc, or ye'll get none o' this 'ere bacon."

Thomas and Joseph had moved closer, intending to sit on two large logs near the fire but, as soon as they had approached the food, the lurcher had slunk closer still, growling, staring and baring his teeth. Now, they stood frozen to the spot, unable to move at all.

"He finks yer after his bit o' grub… Charc! Sit! Stay!"

The lurcher sat and stayed near to Sprig. The apprentices sat and stayed on the other side of the cooking pot and Sprig, well away from the dog.

"Oh, he'll be all right wi' vee once 'e gets to know yer. So, friends, wha' are yer names, an' 'ow come yer a visitin' vis ole charcoal burner, eh?"

"I'm Thomas."

"An' I'm Joseph."

"Well, Thomas, if you'd like to get a couple o' plates an' forks from that ole tent under vem willows, I reckon I can start divvyin' up vis grub… Ee'yar, Charc."

Sprig had fished out one of the rashers with his knife and flicked it across to the dog who tentatively sniffed it then pawed it on the ground, trying to cool it down before chewing pieces from it. Suddenly, there was a cry of, "Oh, my sweet Lord!" and Charc, Sprig and Joseph all turned to look at the shadowy entrance to the large canvass tent that had swallowed Thomas.

Unable to see anything clearly inside the gloom, Thomas was feeling among piles of assorted clothes, pots and pans, wooden boxes, staves and sharp implements that took up most of the floor space. When one of the piles of clothing on the bed decided to move, utter a curse and say, "'Ere, what's vee abart?"

it was all that poor Tommy could do to stay on his feet and not faint away.

The 'pile of clothes' was a little old man with a very long grey beard who had the same stare as Sprig. Tommy rushed back to the fire empty-handed. Charc glared at him, licking his lips, bacon gone.

"There's an old man sat on the bed," he said, pointing a shaking finger at the tent.

"Oh, right. Is 'e awake then?" said the charcoal burner. "Tha's my old dad. 'E don' say much these days—not since me bruvver was took by the consumption... Few monfs back it were..."

Sprig got up, said, "Stay, Charc," and returned a few seconds later with tin plates and forks. Deep in thought now, he doled out roughly equal shares of the pot contents. Then, rousing himself from his dark thoughts, said, "Old feller's not hangry as usual, so we best tuck in, eh. I calls it babble 'n' squeak—but wivout any cabbage. Hee, hee, hee."

With appetites reduced a little, the boys began to eat their meal, very conscious of the dog's plaintive whines and pleading looks.

"Can I give him a bit of my bacon, Sprig?"

"Yer surely can, young Tommy, an' Charc'll be mate's wiv yer ven, I'll wager."

When Thomas threw a small morsel he'd bitten off to the dog, Joseph followed suit. With hardly a chew from Charc, the bacon was swiftly swallowed and the pleading look returned. "Oh, he'd eat the lot if I let 'im. Apples an' turnips an' all," said Sprig. Then, pointing, he commanded the dog, "Charc! Tent!" The lurcher got to his feet and cheerfully trotted off to join the old man in the gloomy tent.

"We've 'ad 'im for years an' 'e's good company for vee ole feller, see... Sat togevver they did, fru the days—an' nights, when I 'ad ter get some shuteye... Watchin' me little bruvver, Ashley. Ash we allas called 'im... Corfin' up blood 'e was; an' night sweats... Terrible business 'twere... Abart your age 'e were, Joe... Gorn ter meet 'is maker, they says."

"We're sorry for your loss, Sprig. Ain't we, Tommy?"

"Yes," said Thomas. "I'll say a prayer for him tonight, one that we learned in church."

"Well, that's real Christian o' vee, Lad. I'm finkin' we'd best cheer up, eh. An' a nice 'ot cuppa rosey lee is the best way ter do it, eh?"

Before drinking his cup of tea, Thomas offered to take the cup meant for Sprig's father to the tent. He wanted to say sorry for disturbing him and check that Charc was now his friend. The elderly man said nothing in response to the apology but gladly accepted the tea with a single nod; the lurcher licked the back of Tommy's hand and stayed by the man's side.

"An' I'll be sayin' a prayer tonight for your son, Ash," was Tommy's parting comment. He thought he'd discerned a slight lifting of the old man's eyebrows and was happy with that.

Over the next thirty minutes, the apprentices said a little of their journey from Manchester and their intended destination. Sprig was amused to hear that, apart from two nights when they had crept into a barn, they had slept on a barge, in a potter's cottage and under the stars on fine nights. The trio agreed that watching the sun rise, or set, or to lie on your back counting the stars in the heavens, were all fine ways to rest a tired body; and the best way to thank God for being alive pondering on your lot in life. Sprig then told them about watching the sunset from the nearby Dunstable Downs because then they would be able to catch a view of London in the far distance if they looked south.

"What's that for, Sprig?" asked Joseph indicating the smoking muddy mound with his thumb. The boys had been impatient to know more since first meeting the charcoal burner. He explained that inside the mound was a carefully arranged pile of seasoned timber surrounding the tinder of dry leaves, shavings and faggots right in the centre. He had covered most of the wood with the turves and soil before lighting the central fire and once he was sure it was burning well added more turves to control how much air reached the timber.

"Dependin' 'ow much timber's inside, it can take free or four days, e'en a week to finish it orf. Yer can't let it burn proper like or ye just finish up wi' ash, instead o' yer charcoal, see... Aye, ash... Funny vat, now 'e's gorn."

Sprig told them that Ashley was twelve years younger than himself and that their mother had died giving birth to him. Since then, his dad had hoped to build up the charcoal business with the three of them running it. Ashley had just reached the stage where they could leave him setting up a new stack while Sprig and his father transported their products to the various iron smelters and markets around the county, but then his consumption became more serious. His father had withdrawn from life ever since they'd lost Ash. Nowadays, Sprig also relied on his coppicing of oak, ash and beech trees for an income; the increased competition from coking coal was fast displacing the demand for charcoal from metal producers. So, he had to sell fencing poles, clothes props and pegs and thatching spars.

"An' I do a bit o' bit of pollarding darn by the river when I can. Alder, willow or hazel—all good for reeds and spokes in the way o' basket weaving." He paused, thinking. "O' course, sweet chestnuts are right good for eatin' as well as makin' canes an' poles for fences."

"What do they look like, Sprig? Can we eat 'em now?" Thomas knew that it would not be long before his hunger pangs would return.

"Leaves are like the fingers o' yer han' but shaped like spears, an' the nats are in lickull shells as like hedgehogs—all spiky like. Floor o' the woods'll be covered in 'em afore long, Mate."

"What they taste like?"

"Best roastin' 'em, Tommy. Warm an' sweet they are ven— lovely grub!"

Joseph had an idea during this conversation.

"Dost think we could buy some of your products, like pegs and staffs, Sprig? Only when we reach London, we could sell 'em an' make a bit o' money for ourselves in the markets, I reckon. Make out we're coppicers or something."

Thomas took out his half-crown and said, "We can pay with this."

"Right, now, you lads, 'arken to me. If yer wanna be alive when yer meets yer ma—don't go flashin' yer cash abart. Vaire's folks in Lon'on, rogues, as cat yer froat for vat much manny. Jus' take art a penny or two a time from yer pocket, see. I'll change vat for vee if ye like. I've got a few coppers an' tanners. An', I've jus' 'ad anuvver o' me bright idees."

He got up, cleared his throat, spat in the fire and went to the tent. Sprig's bronchitic rasp struggled through his damaged larynx, evidence of his own inhalation problems through breathing acidic wood smoke over three decades of charcoal burning. They heard him say, "Art aright', Dad? I've got a couple o' vem nice goose eggs for later. Yer likes vem don' ya?" A gruff grunt was the response.

When Sprig returned he had Charc by his side and the dog ran to Tommy, licked his hand then sat beside him looking up with adoring eyes. Sprig chuckled.

"What I'd tell ya? Anyways, Joe, try this on for size."

He gave Joseph a long fustian coat, sootied but neither as long nor as worn as his own. It fitted him.

"It was Ashley's. 'E weren' a bean pole like me, more your sort o' build an' it'd be a good disguise for ye in case yer gets a nosey constable in vem marke' places, see. Wha' d'yer reckon?"

Thomas and Joseph looked from one to the other and agreed it was a good idea. The charcoal burner went to the hand cart and returned with some pegs, fence staves and canes which he quickly tied together in a single bundle. Then he sat down again and counted out eighteen pennies and two sixpenny coins from a tin he'd fetched from the tent, dropping the pile of coins into one of the coat's long pockets.

"So, if ye gives me vat half-a-crown, my friend, ven ye can enter Lon'on as a pair o' coppicers an' burners, eh? Oh, aye, an' one more fing."

He returned from the tent again with a small hessian bag full of small pieces of charcoal and gave it to Thomas.

"Nar, the pair o' vee 'as got cloves pegs, posts an' charcoal—some wares ter sell."

Thomas gave Sprig his silver coin then reached into the fustian coat pocket and took out the two sixpences and offered them saying, "We won't accept any of this unless you keep payment for it. That's right isn't it, Joe?"

"True as I'm stood here in Ashley's coat, Pal."

"It's too much, lads, but… 'Ere take this tanner an'…" He could see how determined the boys were so gave Joseph one sixpence back and said, "Now, gimme free o' vem pennies an' ven, we're square—all right? Deal?"

Each boy held out his hand and the deal was sealed when Sprig shook both. Then he led them back to main road where he left them making their way to the fresh water brook and thence to Chalk Hill.

From the top of Chalk Hill, the apprentices faced the setting sun and stuck out both their arms from their sides. Thomas was reminded first of Christ on the cross and then of his own promise to say a prayer for Ash.

Walking up the hill their conversation had turned to the subject of scavenging under spinning mules, which both boys had done when they had started work at Quarry Bank Mill. At that time the younger children, armed with hand brushes, were small enough to crawl beneath the twisting threads of drawn cotton humming above their heads.

"I hated that job, Joe," Thomas had said, wheezing as he climbed through tangles of heather and thistles.

"Aye, me too, Tommy. Couldn't wait to get on to doffing instead. Once the brush was clogged up with cotton fluff from the floor you were putting more of it back onto the mule beam than you were taking off... Yeah, hated it I did."

"I was always sick after me shift, Joe. Swallowing fluff from rovings stopped me from feeling so hungry all the time... but when I couldn't breathe properly and all... Me head was splitting fair to make me eyes pop out!"

"Worst of it all, pal, was if you rubbed your eyes and got the fluff in 'em," said Joe. "Used to stick me head in the horse trough o' rain water when the masters weren't looking. Better than leeches or poultices I reckoned. What about you, mate?"

"Aye, Jason told me about that. He weren't so bad was Jason,' replied Tommy. Then they had stopped at the summit of Chalk Hill and turned to the sunset."

Joseph said, "Right, now then, Sprig said the left hand is pointing south and the right hand is pointing north."

Before his companion could say it again that he was confused about left and right, Joseph said, "Turn to the left and London will be afacin' us straight ahead." With that he turned immediately and Tommy did the same, having cast a crafty glance at Joe. He pointed towards a far away, hazy collection of roofs and dim lights.

"So, that there is where we're agoin' is it, Joe?"

"Well, looks like it, Pal. Lucky it's a warm night again cus unless we find another barn or old cowshed, we're sleepin' out in the open tonight."

Due to the time of year, a distant mist and their left turn not quite covering the required number of angular degrees, they were not seeing London. It was more likely to be St Albans but the general direction was correct.

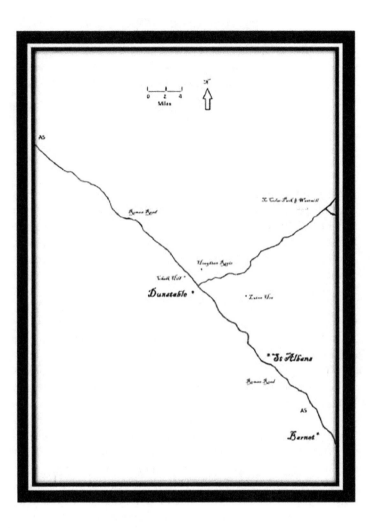

Chapter 8
Barnet via St Albans

Early next morning, they ascended the small climb once more as Thomas needed more reassurance about the direction they were about to travel. They sat together on Chalk Hill sharing their few bruised apples, looking at the vista and musing on life, with Thomas doing most of the talking. He had noticed more estates in the distance by spotting their large mansion houses: Luton Hoo and Houghton Hall.

"I don't know, Joe, why don't we live in them houses? What we got to hide from the rich people for? We ain't criminals; we ain't done nothin' wrong—'cept wantin' to see our mothers. It don't seem right somehow… Don't seem right."

"I keeps tellin' thee, Pal. They've got indentures on both of us, an' that means we can't just up an' leave our jobs. It ain't legal, like. They can arrest us for breakin' the law, see."

"Aye, well I can see that but I don't remember signin' no 'dentures or contracts like Matt said… An' who's law is it as says thee can't go an' visit yer own ma? No, 'tain't right, not at all. An' if that's the law it needs changin' cus it's wrong."

"I agree with thee, Tommy, but we're stuck wi' it an' that's why we gotter be careful like Matt an' Sprig told us. Maybe folks like Matt will be them as get the law changed to be more fair to us poor workin' fellers, eh?"

"Aye, I s'pose yer right, Joe. An' maybe we won't be so poor then… Maybe we can be the ones as get the laws changed, eh?"

Joseph let out a scornful laugh. "Folks like us changin' the law? That's gunner be a lot 'arder than thee thinks, Tommy. About as easy as piecin' porridge, like old Richard Bamford, me gaffer'd say… Aye; nigh on impossible, tha knowst."

"But if Matt thinks blokes like thee an' me—an' him an' 'is mates—can get together an'… Well, I fancy tryin', like, when I'm grow'd a bit more."

"'Eh up, Pal, don't be getting' above thy place, as they keeps tellin' us int' mill. That's what they calls wishful thinkin'. Hee, hee! Thee an' me change the law? That'll be the day, Tommy, that'll be the day…"

Unfortunately, their early camaraderie was not to last long and the two friends spent many of the next few hours either arguing with each other, or running into nearby scrubland or forest to avoid the possible interest from others on the drovers road. There was a constant interruption on the road caused by large groups of men, sometimes accompanied by dogs or large herds of cattle.

Thomas was once again uneasy about failing to attend a church to pray for God's forgiveness on Sunday. Once again, he was convinced that by worshipping properly, in God's house, then such respectful behaviour would be sure to invite the Lord's guiding hand and protection. Joseph became very irritated by his companion's devotion and faith, and eventually refused to listen to Thomas' various schemes. These were intended to make them appear washed, clean and tidy enough to avoid the gaze of local worshippers when entering their church.

It was only after they had hidden for the third time that Sunday and had gathered mud, leaves and collections of various creepers and crawlers from the invertebrate world about their appearance, that Thomas realised it was a hopeless objective. They'd lost much time when they arrived, exhausted and frustrated, in the evening on the outskirts of a village they mistakenly thought could be London. Sheltering under the leaky roof of an old cowshed, the apprentices resolved their differences while chewing the few food scraps they found at the bottom of their sacks. Sleep overtook them before the sun had set that evening.

On Monday morning, it took the runaway apprentices twenty minutes to reach Marshals Wick village, on the outskirts of St Albans, where they were still convinced that they were entering London. As they confidently wandered into the marketplace, they approached a stall selling cold pies, cakes and bread. Joseph gave the stallholder his money for the food they'd bought and casually asked, "Which part o' London are we in, Mate? Only I'm looking to sell some these 'ere pegs an' fence posts, see, an' I can't see any o' them kind o' stalls."

The man had a very red face and was very round in the body, the strings of his apron just about circled his ample middle.

"Aye, I fought vee were strangers, Lad. Thee must o' wandered orf da Lon'on road. Nah, nah, this 'ere's Marshals Wick, ten minutes away from Sen Albans i' is. Take tha' bit of a track o'er yonder for Sen Albans and yer back on the Lon'on road. Bat Lon'on? Nah, nah, that's still a good way orf yet, son. Twenny mile mebbee."

He indicated the path with a nod of his head and a wave of his hand then turned to his next customer. "Nah ven, what can I do for thee, me darlin'? Usual? Cottage loaf an' free o' vem laverly scones is it?"

Joseph thought it best not to mention that they had lost their way a little when diving into the nearby woods again, earlier that morning. The hunt for an escaped prisoner from St Albans' jail had resumed and the men with dogs were widening the search. Their shouts and the hounds' barking alerted the boys long before they'd had a chance to see them.

The two sat for a while, to eat their pies near a market stall selling cheap cutlery that was adjacent to the path they would take. They said little being tired and not wanting to attract attention. But the young man attending the stall had noticed their weary looks and appearance and approached them.

"How do, friends. Yer looks as though yer could do wi' not 'avin' ter carry them heavy loads… 'Ow much for the pegs an' posts? I reckon I could shift 'em from me stall if I tried."

The apprentices had thought that the larger items would help their disguise as coppicers and would be needed when in London. Now that they had discovered they were still so far away from their destination, each had unspoken doubts regarding selling the posts and canes. However, it occurred to Joseph that it would be good not to carry two of their extra packages, indeed they may be in need of some more money during the coming miles. Joseph thought quickly and did a rapid calculation about the nine pence spent with Sprig between all their purchases.

"Well, Tommy, Pal, we must hang on to them canes an' posts for our special customer in London. But we could let this feller 'ave the charcoals an' pegs, doancher think?"

Thomas was completely baffled for a few seconds but when Joseph turned away from the young man and winked, he nodded, knowingly. Now, he became the wise businessman.

"Oh, yes, Joseph. The London customer might become very discontent with us if we were to arrive without his goods. What do you think is a good price for them high quality wooden items?"

The young man was not fooled. Joseph felt a small twinge of panic and confusion at Thomas' strange way of phrasing things and it was the first time he had ever called him 'Joseph'. He smiled at the young man and said, "Sixpence for the pegs an' the bag o' charcoal, Pal?"

"Four."

"Six."

"Four."

"How does… Five sound?

"Done—five it is if yer frow in two canes."

Joe looked at Tommy who pulled a wry face and nodded. "Righto, Pal. Tha's got a good deal, there."

They exchanged goods and money while Thomas nipped back to the pie man to buy two more meat pies. He felt acutely nervous all of the ten minutes it took him, feeling that many of the passers-by and people chatting in small groups were watching him. On this occasion, he was wrong to feel so, as most of the market crowd were too busy to pay much attention to a pair of grubby and sooty young travellers. But before another week had passed, there would be two parish officials, alerted by a letter from Samuel Greg, on the lookout for two young travellers—strangers in the vicinity of Hackney workhouse. Hackney workhouse accommodated almost 280 inmates and was falling into a state of disrepair caused by a lack of maintenance over several years. The board of trustees had failed in its proper management but new plans were being prepared for future improvements. The receipt of a letter from such an eminent business man as Samuel Greg was to result in immediate actions. After all, there was a good chance that Mr Greg might show his gratitude for their assistance by financially supporting some of the much needed—and expensive—improvements.

The parish minister asked his churchwarden and his assistant overseer to select fifteen children who would be suitable workers in the Greg's mill, the upkeep of the poor being such a drain on the parish finances. A letter had been sent by return to Samuel Greg stating as much: '… and if you are in want of any young apprentices at Quarry Bank, we could readily furnish you with a dozen or more as from nine to twelve years of age of both sexes… '

***

When Thomas and Joseph had found their way back onto the road to London, it was also to discover they were quite quickly in the midst of St Albans where very little industry was taking place. They had passed by a few very wet-looking fields growing water cress on the way in but the town centre seemed to be full of numerous old inns, it being the first coaching stop to and from England's capital. As an ancient site of Christian pilgrimage, the town had an aura of piety and deep religiosity which, had the boys known, would have re-kindled their recent argument about corrective worship. This did not occur since their accidental happening upon St Albans prison, just prior to midday, had the opposite effect of inducing an affliction of dumbness in both young men. This ailment was accompanied by the remarkable ability to walk at such an increased rate that there was a strong likelihood they would catch up with the noonday stagecoach as it left the White Swan Inn bound for London. There was a silent agreement between the two alarmed minds that St Albans was not for them.

At around four o'clock, they arrived without incident on the outskirts of Chipping Barnet, a place with a long history of philanthropy, alms houses and schools for the poor of the parish. Barnet Fair and Market was coming to a close and as Joseph was still eager to try and dispose of their wares, they wandered about the market place curious to find a suitable stall. The plan was then to use their disguise while asking for directions to Hackney.

"Look, Joe that stall has all kinds of wooden things, chairs and benches—even fence posts and clothes props."

110

"Righto, Tommy let's give it a try, eh?"

The two men in charge of the stall were busy loading up two horse-drawn carts with their products, creating a precarious pile in each and tying it down securely with ropes. They were both keen to start off home and get their supper, not having had a very profitable day they were in a grumpy mood.

"Afternoon, Mate," said Joseph, quite as cheerfully as his tiredness, hunger and thirst allowed. "Can I interest thee in buying some o' these top quality fence posts an' walking canes for the infirm?"

One of the two robust and hirsute men carried on loading up the carts, pausing briefly to shake his head in a despairing manner, having looked the apprentices up and down with a scathing glance. His partner and elder brother gave the pair a similar look, sucked his few remaining teeth and said, "Nah where on God's earf 'ave you two cam from? Yer've lef' it a bit late, my son. We're orf 'ome nah, ain't we? Done very li'ul business today, so, wha' would I be wantin' more stuff for? Carnt sell what we got already."

"Right, I see. I just wondered, like. Thanks for yer time, Pal... Erm, can you put us on the right road to Hackney then?"

Thomas had wandered away to look at a nearby stall selling bottles of spring water from Ye Old Physic Well. He was being persuaded about its health-giving benefits and thought of buying a bottle for Joseph who was still suffering stomach cramps from time to time.

The younger stallholder of wooden goods stopped loading, scratched his head and said to his brother, in a rather doubtful manner, "Hmm, I suppose we might find a bit o' room for a couple o' them canes, Jake. Councillor Burrell was arsking 'bout one for 'is ol' farver today."

Jake nodded wisely and asked Joseph, "I can take two o' them walkin' canes, friend, so 'ow much?"

"Four pence, Pal. But... If you take half of 'em 'ow does, say, ten pence sound?"

"Hmm, I dunno, Son... 'Ow many's half a bandle of 'em then?"

"We've got a dozen left to sell so you'd be taking six."

Jake pursed his lips, flicked a look at his brother, Johnny, then at the carts. "Four pence for two, eh—bu' ten pence for six?"

"You've got it, Pal. So, what d'yer say?"

"Nah, I'll get 'em cheaper orf me usual bloke tomorrer."

Jake joined Johnny loading up the carts as Thomas came back to remind Joseph about asking for the directions to Hackney. Then he said, "I think we should buy a bottle o' that spring water, Joe. He claims it'll sort out all kinds of ailments, including your belly ache."

"I dunno, Tommy. We might need our bit o' cash for when we reach Hackney. Probably don't work any road, Pal."

Hearing this conversation Johnny said, "Nah, Son, it's good staff. Folks rarnd 'ere swears by it for many a year. Stops yer belly ache, rheuma tiz an' all sorts. It has wha' they calls coorativ proper'ies, Mate… S'right ain't it, Jake?"

"Oh, aye, Son. True as ye stood there i' is. Sam famous polly teeshun… Gavvermen' man 'e were… 'E swore by its proper'ies 'e did… Wrote it all darn in 'is books."

"Yeah, Joe, that's what the feller on the stall told me. I couldna read his name—summat like Peppers, Christian name same as old Greg's, Joe—Samuel. Said you'd need two bottles, one for yer belly an' one for bowels he reckoned. It might stop us coughin', as well."

Joseph was now intrigued enough to ask, "An' 'ow much is it, Tommy?"

"Tuppence a bottle. I've come back to see what ye think?" Joseph looked surprised and very doubtful.

"That's a lot o' money, Tommy. Might be best to wait till we get to Hackney, might be cheaper there, as well, see."

Jake stopped loading his cart, wandered nearer to the apprentices and said in lowered tones, "Look 'ere, my friends, I like the look o' the pair o' thee, so I fink I've got a scheme what might do us bofe a bit o' good. Tommy 'ere is quite correc' abart that famous feller, Samuel Peppers. Since 'e wrote 'is books folks cams from miles ararnd ter buy them bockulls o' physic. But oi can take yer to the source o' that there spring water—not far from 'ere is it, Johnny?"

"Nah, Jake's right abart that, Mate." He pointed. "It's darn there, darn Wood Street an' along the Well'ouse Lane. Ah tells

112

thee, the folks rarnd 'ere, they jus' goes an' fills up as many bockulls as they likes, see."

Joseph was not a little suspicious at whatever scheme Jake was about to reveal but decided to listen.

"An' what's this plan o' yourn, Pal? How we s'posed to profit by it?"

"I dare say yer've got a couple o' water bockulls each in them sacks yer carryin'—right?" They nodded. "An', if yer fills 'em up from that Old Well pamp in the field ah takes thee to, then ye'll 'ave a lot more physic water, free! Loads, freer than two cossly bockulls o' the staff—right?" They nodded again, their foreheads now furrowed with puzzlement.

"We've got one or two more empty water bockulls thee can 'ave, as well, I dare say. S'right innit, Johnny?" Now Johnny nodded, slightly frowning, equally unsure of his brother's plan. "Well, my friends, if we gives the pair o' thee a lift to that pamp, in the field darn Well'ouse Lane, an' then we drops yer bofe orf on the 'ackney road... Well, stands ter reason dunnit? Yer've got all the medicine yer needs an'—an'—yer ganner be a few miles along on the right road ter Lon'on."

"So," drawled Joseph, "what do you get out o' all this?"

"All o' yer bandle o' walkin' canes for a shillin'. That's the top an' bottom on it... What d'yer say?"

"But that's twelve canes for twelve pennies, innit?" Thomas could see the proposition even though his arithmetic was not a strength he was proud of. Joseph spoke to Jake.

"Give us a few seconds to talk about it, Pal."

The brothers continued loading up their carts while the apprentices walked a short distance away to talk.

"Joe, you was askin' for tuppence for each cane, but he wants all of 'em for a penny each? 'Ow is that a good deal?"

"Look, Mate, Sprig let us 'ave the bloomin' lot for nine pence—everythin', pegs, charcoal, posts an' walkin' canes. We got five pence last time, from that other bloke. If we add this feller's twelve pence, that's seventeen, nearly double what we paid, Tommy. An' we still got all the fence posts ter sell later on. Whatever we get for them, Pal, it's all a tidy profit, ain't it?"

This was just a little too much arithmetic for Thomas to cope with, so he replied, "If you say so, Joe. I'll allas trust thee ter do the right thing, Pal… An' I s'pose we get a lift a few more miles along on the right road as well, eh?"

"An' that's the most important thing of all, Tommy. An' we might sell some o' this 'ere physic water that we don't drink. Who knows, eh…? We're so close to our mothers now, Tommy, we gotter go for this."

"Righto, Pal."

Joseph walked up to Jake and said, "Make it one an' tuppence, Pal, an' yer've got a deal—cus we'll 'elp thee to finish loadin' up the carts."

He stuck out his hand to shake on the deal. Jake smiled; he was beginning to take to this likeable young man, this young entrepreneur.

"One an' a penny, Joe."

"Hmm… Right you are, Jake. It's a deal, Pal."

They shook hands and the two runaways began to assist the brothers with their loading. The first items that Thomas loaded were all of the walking canes, so glad was he not to be carrying them as well as his sacks.

In 1664 and 1667, Samuel Pepys visited Chipping Barnet and on each occasion, he drank some of the water from the Old Physic Well. After taking five glasses of it, on the first visit, he wrote about his journey home: '… My waters working at least seven or eight times upon the road, which pleased me well… ' When he returned three years later, he 'took only three glasses then went to the Red Lyon… ' where he '… ate some of the best cheese cakes I ever did eat in my life'.

Unknown to Thomas and Joseph, it was thought that the main property of the spring water was its likely diuretic effects on the system. Since both of the travelling absconders later sampled it several times, on their final walk to Hackney, their frequent stops for similar relief of their bladders along the way would have seemed to confirm the theory.

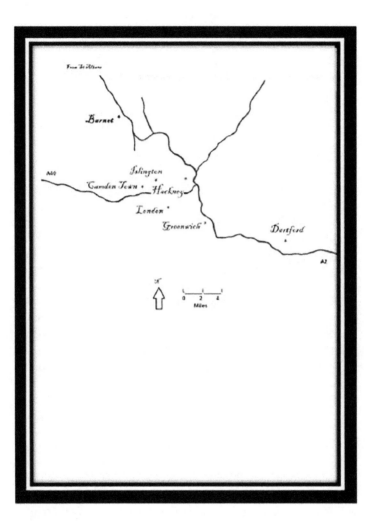

Chapter 9
Finding Old Friends

Even though it was now the first few days of a warm July, the travellers' joints felt stiff and they ached in the neck and shoulders. The previous night had been cold and the novelty of sleeping out in the open was wearing thin. They had walked for half of the day and had used up some of their money buying food along the way. Joseph's fustian coat had seemed to grow heavier with every potential customer's refusal to buy his fence posts. Attracting suspicious looks from curious passers-by was making the two boys nervous once more and irritation between them was also creeping up to cast an air of pointless resentment. When they had unknowingly wandered away from the main road and into the parish of Islington, Joseph stopped suddenly and looked around him.

"Tommy, I know that old church there. I used to go there with me ma, when I were just a nipper... Aye, learned all about little baby Jesus—in 'is crib an' that... "

Joseph looked into the distance for a few seconds as memories drifted back to him. Then he suddenly became excited and dumping the bundle of fence posts on the ground, ran to the wall around the cemetery. From the top, where he'd climbed, he waved an arm in a southerly direction and added, "Aye, Tommy. An' over that way is the Green; Clerkenwell Green they calls it but I never ever saw no green grass there, Pal. Hee, hee, that's 'ow come I remembers it, see. Cus there ain't no grass there. Well..."

"What we gonner do now then, Joe? I wouldn't mind restin' a bit."

Joseph jumped down from the wall and considered throwing the coat and the posts over it and into the cemetery. A gentleman accompanying two women passed them by and Joe changed his mind when the man paused to regard the boys warily. Whatever the man thought, he kept to himself and the three continued their stroll. Fear of insurrection from the lower and working classes was quite prevalent amongst the landowners and middle classes of Britain during the early decades of the 19th century. This was as a result of the wars with Napoleon and the horrors of the French Revolution just a few miles across the Channel. There had been violent reactions to the Acts of land enclosure, as well as much physical opposition to the machines, of people like Richard Arkwright and Samuel Crompton, which had put many of the working classes out of a job. Rumours of riots, news of invasion of the properties of these entrepreneurial inventors and their machines being smashed by angry mobs, had spread throughout the land.

"I think if we follow that road across the way, Tommy, we'll come to Shoreditch on the way to Hackney. But if we go in the opposite direction, we might come to Clerkenwell where I was born. Might see some neighbours of me mother. Who knows, eh?"

Looking very crestfallen, Thomas said, "That's all right for you, Mate, but I ain't got no idea about 'ow to find where my ma lived. We was in the workhouse when I was but a nipper, as well."

"Don't fret, Tommy, we know you were born in Gray's Inn Lane, so we can find it, eh? I've got a feelin' it ain't far from Clerkenwell. If we ask at a few doors while it's still light could be we'll find someone that remembers your mother or mine."

The two decided to find their way to the district of Clerkenwell and seek old acquaintances of their parents. What neither of them knew at that moment was that near to the centre of the old village of Clerkenwell stood the first of two very imposing buildings, each of which would strike fear in the apprentices' hearts. The second building would be Hackney workhouse, more often called the Poor House, and still the residence of Mrs Priestley. Whereas the edifice near to Joseph's 'Green', known locally as the Old Sessions, had the more formal title of the Middlesex Sessions House. Therein they would later meet clerks of the court, official witnesses and one very unsympathetic Justice of the Peace.

* * *

The gathering gloom of twilight was beginning to frighten Thomas when they began to knock on the doors of the many old houses along Frog Lane. They had slowly worked their way along two streets that ran off Clerkenwell Green. Lower Street joined with Cross Street and many of the houses they had tried there were not in a good state of repair. A Mr Tufnell who owned many of those properties had agreed to sell them to a Mr Cannon whose plan, unknown to the current residents, was to demolish them in favour of commercial offices and shops. Those tenants that deigned to open their doors to the exhausted boys either began the conversation with a brusque refusal to buy the fence posts they carried or shook their heads when asked if they had knowledge of a Mrs Priestley or a Mrs Sefton. It was not so much the gloom that scared Thomas as the characters who began to populate the streets at dusk.

It seemed to Thomas that on every street corner there were gathered two or three very dirty and shifty-looking men. Their grime had more of a festering look than the dirt of dusty roads, such as clothed the runaway travellers. But it was the predatory glint in their eyes that shocked Thomas and he whispered his concerns to Joseph.

"Aye, Tommy, I've noticed 'em already. If they tries anythin' then one o' these fence posts is gonner be a club, no worries, Pal."

"I think I'd rather be away from 'ere as soon as you like, Joe." Thomas separated a post for himself and hugged it to his scrawny body.

"Me an' all, Mate," agreed Joseph. "We'll just try a couple more o' these old doors, eh. Then we can go back to the churchyard, maybe doss down there."

The thought of sleeping in a cemetery did very little to improve the boy's courage and as he pondered on that idea, Joseph tapped a very battered old door with his new 'club'. The wooden door panels and its frame were splintered, scratched and split. The function of keeping out cold winter draughts was a long lost cause and so the elderly married couple inside had to make do with its doubtful ability to keep out unwanted visitors.

A shaky voice, of indeterminate gender, was heard to shout: "Who's there? What o' yer a wantin' at this time o' night?"

Gambling on the voice belonging to an old man, Joseph asked, "I'm right sorry to be disturbin' yer, Sir, but would you be knowin' the whereabouts of a Mrs Sefton? She used to live around these parts but fell on 'ard times when 'er 'usband went off to fight in the war."

There was a pause and then low mumbling voices could be heard through the cracks in the door panels. They were sure that another more female tone was involved and this voice replied, "And what might be the Christian name o' this 'ere Mrs Sefton?"

Joseph's eyebrows were raised at this first tentatively positive response. "Why she was known as Esther; Essy to 'er friends, tha knowst."

"And who might thee be? Yer not from rarnd these parts, wi' speechifyin' like that, are ye?"

The locals on the corner of the street had noticed the boys and Thomas saw how their attention was directed at them. He called out, "This is 'er son—Joseph. Mrs Sefton's son, Joseph Sefton—all the way from Manchester, see."

There was a short gasp from each of the apprentices when an inquisitive eye appeared at the largest crack in the door panel. The female voice demanded, "Stand in front 'ere where I can see ye."

After a slight shuffling about on the doorstep outside, a sigh and more muffled discussion on the inside of the door, there was suddenly a great clattering and clunking of bolts, followed by a clinking of brass locks and keys. The old door swung slowly open to reveal a tall but bent old man and his small but bright elderly wife. They were well-dressed in good quality but faded clothes of an earlier fashion.

"Well, well, young Joseph Sefton, ye best come in afore it gets too dark to see your handsome young face."

So, saying the lady of the house reached out both hands and waved the boys inside. She stepped to one side to allow them space to enter. While the trio moved to the sparsely furnished but neat and tidy living room, her husband locked up the front door once more.

"And who's this fine fellow yer've brought with ye?" she asked, indicating two wooden chairs for them to sit upon.

Darkness had fallen by the time the apprentices had reluctantly revealed as much of their travels as they'd dared to Rachel and Arthur Payne. They had known Joseph when he was a baby and known Essy, his mother, from then until recent times. She had gone into service 'somewhere in Boe-voyer Tarn on this side o' the river' according to Arthur. Of his father, John, they knew nothing more than Joseph and said they had assumed he had been lost in the Napoleonic wars. Gratefully clutching hot cups of sweet tea, after consuming two of Rachel's freshly baked currant buns, the boys were eager to hear about the unfortunate events that had befallen Joe's mother.

Over the ten years or more since Mrs Sefton had first been admitted to the Poor House, she had occasionally been able to secure employment as a scullery maid in nearby respectable households. Now that she was older, she had found it difficult to be employed similarly, since that duty was most often performed by the youngest of the servants. Rachel and Arthur had often given shelter to Essy for short periods of time.

Their sympathy arose partly from when they had been neighbours in Frog Lane; and also because their own three children had died from an outbreak of cholera. But she had spent most of the years, when Joseph had been working in Styal, working as a drudge in Hackney workhouse. He listened in complete silence, hot tears running down his ruddy cheeks.

"Now then, young Joseph, I've got something to tell ye that may well add to yer sadness."

She sighed deeply, glanced at her husband as if to receive his permission and then he spoke directly to Joseph himself.

"Ye may well be as 'appy as Larry wi' one bit o' news, lad… But be cast down into the depths wi' the other bit o' news what Rachel 'as got for ye."

Now he looked to his wife for permission when he said, "Tell thee what, Rachel, but a little drop o' gin or brandy in that cup o' tea might perk 'em up a speck. What d'yer say to that, eh?"

Without hesitation, his wife nodded. "Aye, all right, Art. I reckon this would be a right time for't. Go on."

"Which tipple are ye partial to, lads?"

When each young man merely shrugged their shoulders in ignorance, Arthur said, "Well, if ye've not tasted enough alkyhol to 'ave a liking for it, I'd say that was a good sign. Cus it'll cause ye the devil o' problems if ye takes it up too much. Let that be a warning to the pair o' thee, eh."

They said nothing but took a sip of the brandy tea Arthur chose for them on his return from the scullery. Coughing gently, they smiled awkwardly while nodding in approval. Their smiles froze on their faces and swiftly vanished when they heard Mrs Payne's next words.

"Ye could've had two little bruvvers, Joseph... But one of 'em died o' the measles afore he was one year old, poor little mite. Esther was going to take him to the Foundling 'orsepital but it was too late for him."

"But you said me father was lost in the war and she..."

Rachel held up a hand to stop his talking then paused, wanting to get her next words right.

"Your mother fell pregnant when she was in the workhouse but had been working as a scullery maid for nigh on four months afore she found out. They gave Essy her marching orders as soon as they knew in the big house; 'twas over near Knightsbridge Barracks. A shame it were, a real shame as it could've turned out all right for the girl. It was her first job outside o' the workhouse and she was afeared to go back in with the baby so she came back here for a while—till he died. Then I got a fever, miasma the doctor called it, and Arthur wouldn't let her stay. Said she brought it with her from the workhouse and sent her back there..."

"Oh, I felt sorry for yer muvver an' no mistake," interrupted Arthur. "But if it comes darn to choosin' betwixt me missus an' anuvver person, well, it's obvious, ain't it?"

Thomas and Joseph muttered indistinct words of agreement then fell silent again, until Joseph said, "Mrs Payne, you said me ma 'ad two boys born to 'er... So, what about the other little 'un?"

"Little Daniel is still alive as far as we know, Joseph. He's three now and still in the Poor House in the infants quarters."

"But you said me ma was workin' in another big house, somewhere this side of the river. Why isn't the child with her?"

"Esther has a much better position now, Joseph. She's a kitchen maid but they know nothing about her child. And Daniel—"

She looked at her husband who said, "Tell the lad, Rachel. He's a right to know what's 'appening to 'is bruvver, arter all. That's what I think."

"Joseph, Daniel was born in Hackney workhouse and so he became a pauper child. That means they can take 'im from his mother and decide his future. We reckon he'll be apprenticed in a few more years to a trade—maybe a tannery, or a blacking factory…"

"Or maybe in a cotton mill, like us two," finished Joseph.

Later that evening when the four were eating supper, the subject of Thomas' mother came up and he had a chance to express his wish to visit her in the Poor House. The boys had explained the reasons behind their burden of fence posts which were dumped in a corner of a bedroom that Rachel explained they could use for a short time—until they were ready to return to Cheshire. The apprentices had omitted the fact that they had absconded from the mill and, while Rachel had the impression they had permission for a visit, Arthur strongly suspected that they were runaways. He had been a watchman for many years, patrolling streets between nine at night until six the next morning, dealing with all kinds of criminality. He was particularly proud of his ability to sense when he was being told 'a blatant pack o' lies!' but kept these thoughts to himself—for the time being.

Before they all went to bed that night, it had been agreed that the apprentices would attempt to find out more about Tommy's mother by visiting Gray's Inn Lane the next day. Arthur had told them it was less than a mile from Frog Lane and agreed to give them directions to it and to Hackney workhouse, though that was about two or three miles away in the opposite direction. Once again, the two boys had found kindness and were effusive with their expressions of gratitude. Once again, their offers to pay for their keep were refused but later, when alone in their room, the boys counted up their combined cash and agreed they could pay 'thruppence a day' for about another week. If they met with more objections, they planned to hide the sum somewhere in the kitchen where it could be found after they'd departed from London.

"Another thing, Tommy, I'm gettin' real tired o' cartin' these fence posts around without sellin' any on 'em."

As if to emphasise his frustration, Joseph gave the bundle a hefty kick which separated two of the offending pieces of timber and they flew across the floor, hitting the door. The echoing crash resulted in a shout from Arthur disrobing in the other bedroom.

"Every fing all right, lads?"

"Oh, aye, Mr Payne. Everything's… Erm, nice-as-pie, and thanks. I tripped o'er the rug, like."

"Oh, right. G'night, then."

"Thanks for puttin' us up. G'night."

Joseph's eyes looked up to the cracked ceiling and he inwardly cursed himself. Thomas had stuffed his fist into his mouth in an attempt to stifle his giggles. Tears of mirth ran down his cheeks and he received a playful punch to his arm from Joseph who glared at the inanimate pile of posts and muttered, "About as much use to us as a bobbin full o' feathers is to a spinning mule."

Despite their brief good humour and worries about the events of tomorrow, the apprentices fell asleep within minutes of laying their heads on the clean white pillows.

The next three days were spent knocking on doors in the Gray's Inn Lane district for most of the time. At some point in the afternoon, the pair would walk to Hackney determined to ask at the Poor House entrance about Thomas' mother and Joseph's little brother. Each time they'd set off from Gray's Inn Lane, chewing the snack that Mrs Payne had prepared for them, discussing the information gathered that morning and agreeing on what it was best to say once they had been allowed to enter the workhouse. The brilliant summer sunshine encouraged a cheerful jaunt but on each day, they failed to arrive at the main entrance due to a failure of their nerve. They would convince each other of the importance of walking all around the outer walls just to get their 'bearings'.

Climbing onto a neglected cart or discarded wooden crate and glancing over the wall into the stone breaking yard became the most pressing of occupations. Hundreds of tons of Blue Guernsey Granite were delivered every week to the workhouse for the male inmates to break down. Watching the men collect their tools from the shed behind the men's ward and commence the intensely hard labour was somehow of greater urgency. It was a helpful distraction that neither boy would admit to if questioned. They would return to the Payne's simple but slowly dilapidating cottage and respond to their questions with the same negative answers each time. Then on the third day, they had an extra piece of information.

"Aye, me mother's still in the workhouse. No-one knows 'ow long she's been in there… Them as remembers her. One or two folks thought they could remember me as a nipper." Thomas became quiet.

"There was one kind woman, who gave us a drink o' water what told us Tommy's ma has children—in there—with her as well. But…"

"But what, Joseph?" asked Mrs Payne, turning to listen as she lit the candles.

"I don't remember 'aving any brothers or sisters that lived," said Thomas. "They died—both of 'em. It were not long after we was took into the workhouse, see. Dunno what they died from."

Mr and Mrs Payne exchanged knowing looks but asked no more questions. Rachel spoke next with a kindly and sympathetic tone.

"Ye know, boys, a lot o' fings can change o'er just a few years. Joseph here, he reminds me a lot of his pa. But he don't talk like him no more, like he comes from round this part o' London."

"Nah, nah," chipped in Arthur. "No' at all. Neever thee nor young Tommy there. Yer bofe sounds like real norverners. Like some o' them fellers I knows, as come orf the barges… Manchester way, was it?"

Joseph changed the subject.

"Ye know, Mr Payne, I reckon them fence posts'll be more use to you an' Mrs Payne than us. Nobody round 'ere 'as a use for 'em, so if you've got an axe, I could chop 'em up for you as firewood. Most likely save you a bit o' money through this comin' winter. What d'yer say to that then?"

"Well, that's a good idea, Joe," replied Arthur, smiling, aware of what Joe was up to. "It would be better'n chuckin' 'em away, I agree. But ye must take a fair price for 'em."

"No,' said Thomas. "We already talked about it an' agreed to give you the cash if we sold 'em. For us board an' keep, like. It ain't right to stop 'ere for now."

"No, Mr Payne, you must 'ave 'em," insisted Joseph. "But not for money. We want to pay our way. It's only right, Mrs Payne."

He'd turned to Rachel and hoped to get her to agree and convince her husband. But the bent old man had something in mind of his own reasoning and replied first.

"Right y'are, lads. We'll keep 'em; an' I might choose a couple o' posts o' the right shape to nail across me frant door. 'Twould 'elp keep some o' that chill wind art later on." He placed both his hands on his back to straighten up with a slight groan. "Yer can help me do that if yer've a mind."

They both nodded eagerly. Mr Payne then gave each boy an intense and meaningful look before continuing, "Now then, I can see yer 'avin' a bit o' difficulty gettin' fru the front door o' the Poor House. I reckon I can give thee a bit o' 'elp an' advice wi' that. But ye must agree ter let me. Cus I've got one or two fings in mind ter help thee."

Rachel beamed a big smile at her husband. It was a thing that they had discussed about helping the apprentices while the boys were out of their house, walking to Hackney. Arthur had his suspicions about the truth of the situation and had revealed them to his wife, together with a possible solution. They had a kind of proposition to put to the worried young men but it needed to be handled most delicately. Was this ex-watchman the person to do it?

The imposing front of the Hackney workhouse gave the two apprentices such a cause for concern that, yet again and in spite of their promises to their new friends, they immediately abandoned their plan to enter and ask about their mothers. Their bitter disappointment on finding that things had gone very wrong for the women over and again had been hard to bear. Arthur Payne had managed to talk the apprentices into forming ambitions for the future. During their long discussion with the elderly couple, on that prior evening, they had each resolved to learn their trade well enough to become reliable employees of a cotton mill. The exact location of it was still undisclosed. Then they would be more able to set up a home of their own; one where they would hope to support the scattered remnants of their two families.

Joseph's private wish was to one day buy his own farm where he might make a different living raising livestock. His secret fanciful picture included the pretty paintress of porcelain, from Burslem, but he kept that even from Thomas. Thomas wanted nothing more than to live with his mother again; to be the man of the family, taking care of her and the brother and sister of his that he had never met. Arthur had convinced them that by keeping their aims for a better life in front of them, at all times, it would enable them to overcome their fear of a small thing like the main entrance to Hackney workhouse.

This was to be the day the apprentices would stride boldly towards the main entrance as two proud and respectable young men. With a little help from Rachel, they were wearing clean clothes, with faces scrubbed clean and hair plastered neatly down. But yet again, it looked as though they might fail to cover the last fifty yards of their journey. On the way there, Joseph had convinced himself and, therefore, his younger companion that if they were captured, they would suffer the horrors of custody in Newgate prison. Try as they might, they could not construct a story they felt would be good enough to convince any member of the law that all they wished was to see their close kin; Thomas' mother and their younger siblings. Matt's advice to them and also Arthur's, about being truthful, no longer seemed to hold sufficient sway to avoid incarceration.

Instead of entering, they walked around the outer walls again, trying to decide whether they could face the Paynes with the truth of another failed attempt. Watching them from one of the Poor House windows were two burly men. The crowns of their heads were each as clear of hair as the hard-boiled eggs they were enjoying. As if to compensate for this lack of hirsuteness, the men's cheeks displayed a wonderfully bushy pair of mutton chop sideburns. One had whiskers the colour of the yolk of his egg, while the other's set of mutton chops had a hue to match the man's blackened finger nails. They were two bailiffs working for the Board of Trustees and they were on the look-out for Thomas and Joseph. They had been alerted a few days earlier by the workhouse Master, whose house looked out onto Homerton High Street. He and his wife had seen two young men behaving strangely in the vicinity of Hackney workhouse. And now, the bailiffs were sure that the two 'suspicious characters' they could see from their window were the two apprentices that had run away from the northern cotton mill. Details of a letter from Mr Samuel Greg had been disclosed to the men. One boy was older and taller and each was thin and unhealthily pale. The tan the boys had acquired on their trek south added some doubt but the bailiffs had come to a decision. They would arrest them first of all and leave the question of their guilt or innocence to the consideration of the Master of Hackney workhouse and a local magistrate. The bailiffs grabbed their staffs, moved quickly out of the building and ran across Homerton High Street towards the apprentices.

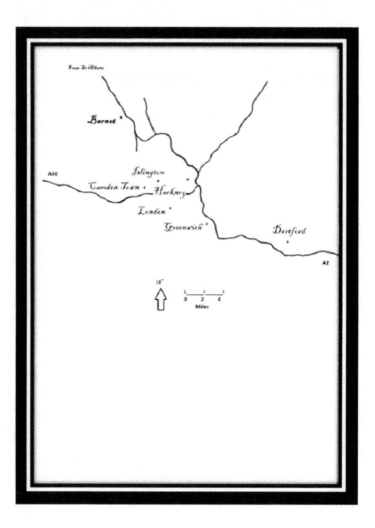

Chapter 10
Hopes and Dreams

"Scarper, Tommy! Run for yer life!" yelled Joseph before the men had taken more than three or four steps in their direction. The bailiffs were well used to pursuing escaping miscreants and ne'er-do-wells of one kind or another and they gave chase. Big and strong they may have been but fleet of foot, they were not.

Their usual cries of: "Stop thief!" and, "Hold them fast!" had little effect other than to turn a few curious heads. Within half a mile, the boys had lost their pursuers by running left and right, back and forth, twisting and turning down various alleyways, leaping over tumble-down walls and stinking streams of sewage. They had to pause for breath eventually when they had reached an area of open countryside, more correctly known as De Beauvoir Town. Here there were very few of the cheaper terraced and tumbledown properties they had left behind them. It was not their usual route back to Frog Lane and hiding in the hedges and copses bordering some of the grand houses along the way reminded both of them about their journey from Styal down to London.

"Where d'yer reckon we are, Joe?"

"Well, Pal, whatever it's called it's a sight more proper than Frog Lane, where we better head for next. Cus I ain't in a rush to be hidin' in 'edges an' ditches again."

"You nor me, Joe." Thomas stared at the large white house, with its ivy-covered walls, in the distance. "Could be your ma is livin' in one o' these posh houses."

"Aye, but we ain't about to knock on the door an' ask, are we? Look at the state o' the pair on us, eh."

It was true that they had acquired much of the local mud and vegetation about their person once more. Their hair had more of the character of a discarded bird's nest than the polished tidiness of earlier that morning. Although the house observed by Thomas was not the one that employed Mrs Sefton as a kitchen maid, there was a grand property, adjacent to the Kingsland Road nearby, where she could be found assisting the cook at that very moment helping to prepare a sumptuous meal for the evening.

By the time the apprentices had found their way back on to the road that led to Frog Lane, it was dark. Rachel had spent much of the day looking out of the bedroom windows hoping that they might return safely. Resisting any similar revelation of fondness towards them, her husband had spent most of his time going through the timber posts, choosing which could be planed down by a joiner he knew. He'd not admit it but he had also looked up and down the streets a few times, when pausing for a conversation on the corner with his neighbours. Then he'd return to the house and attempt to learn a few more words from the three books in his possession, occasionally glancing up and advising Rachel 'not to worry'.

"They made it this far from Manchester all right, so I reckon they knows what they're adoin', gell."

The sun had been set for over an hour before the Paynes heard a knock at their front door. Arthur was the first to be peering through the cracks and confirming it was Thomas and Joseph.

"I fought yer'd get lorst," he said nonchalantly on opening the door. "Cam on in an' tell us yer tale o'er a bit o' supper Rachel as put art for thee."

When they had explained about being chased away from the front of Hackney workhouse, Arthur was curious to know what the men looked like. He maintained that if there was nothing that the boys had done wrong then there was no reason for them to run away. Of course, they still insisted they just wanted to find out more about their relatives and said they'd suspected the men were robbers. But the man with the orange whiskers and bald pate reminded Arthur of a bailiff he had known when he had worked as a watchman on the urban streets. Cautious still, he kept that information to himself, convinced as he was that once the boys knew of his connection with the law, they would flee, never to be seen again. Now that he'd grown to care so much about their well-being Arthur wanted to be sure he had much more of their trust before he revealed his hand.

He was quick to accept the apprentices' decision the next morning about starting on the repairs to the front door. They also announced that they would prefer to explore the area around Mrs Sefton's place of employment before returning to Hackney workhouse. If there was any chance that Joseph could meet her then, naturally, he would welcome it. While the boys were in their backyard sawing up fence posts, Arthur and Rachel had another serious conversation about the situation.

"I knows I could be wrong, Rachel, but I'm certain sure that them two lads is runaways. They're afeared o' being caught an' sent to jail or summat."

"Is that what'll 'appen to 'em, Art—if they gets caught I mean?"

"Nah, I don't fink so, gell. Though, I've known men deported for less; pinchin' ribbons for 'is wife's birthday; or bread for their kids… Usual fing is to take runaways back to their master to finish their apprenticeship, see, an' then they as to take any stick as is comin' their way—for runnin' orf o' course."

"So, what d'yer fink we can do, my dear? I'd love 'em to see their muvvers afore they go back to their Manchester mill."

"That's if it is in Manchester, Rachel. An' what abart Essy Sefton? Might'n it ruin 'er new life in that big house if they just turns up?"

"Oh, it has to be done right… I just fink if it were me, an' I hadn't seen me son for eight years. Me art would burst wi' the joy on it. Such a fine lookin' lad he is now."

"Aye, Rachel, it 'as ter be done right, so I'll be finkin' on it… For now, we might let fings just drift along for a couple o' days then tell 'em what they ought to do, eh?"

"Be careful, we can't make fings worse for their muvvers, Arthur. Just remember that. They got to be made to see that."

"Yes, yes, I know, I know. They gotter 'ave some fings laid art for 'em to make sure their muvvers don't suffer none."

***

The master and matron of Hackney workhouse took their responsibilities for the paupers in their care very seriously.

Trying to manage the discipline and the economy of the institution required a skilful balance between cruelty and kindness. The master always tended to emphasise the former trait since he answered to an Overseer of the Poor who believed that the workhouse was both a place of work and a place of deterrence. His wife, the matron, had the domestic side of things to take care of, as well as any matters that appertained to the female paupers. They had an army of staff to assist them in these duties and this army included cleaners, cooks, porters, washerwomen, scullery maids and chimney sweeps. Much of the work was done by the pauper inmates themselves and casual labour from outside of the institution had to accept poor wages and long hours. Most often, the poor that lived outside of the workhouse kept themselves out of it only by taking on such poorly paid drudgery.

A list of rules and strong discipline did not prevent the workhouse from becoming a noisy and disorderly place where abuse between inmates, both verbal and physical, was common. This often occurred daily during some weeks of the year when too many itinerants added their numbers to the workhouse population. They usually brought with them even more petty crime together with their own particular distress and anxieties from the world outside. The system of sanctions for disobeying the rules or committing various misdemeanours could include reductions in food rations, cells of punishment and beatings, although this last was forbidden for women and girls.

There was an infirmary on the site, exclusively for the Poor House sick, which had two wards. The occupants of the wards were most often those classed as elderly or 'aged', who were also allowed sweet tea to drink rather than the water given to everyone else. The master and matron rarely visited the infirmary because they had no time to familiarise themselves with the needs and wants of the sick.

Butter and sugar for the aged and bread and milk for children under nine were little extras allowed at breakfast time. It was gruel for all others. The able-bodied inmates had a diet that included cooked meat, vegetables, soup, suet pudding, broth, bread and cheese; but all of the food was of a very poor quality and badly prepared. Like the food the work and routine of the workhouse was designed to be boring and unpleasant. The intention was to demoralise, and thus deter people from seeking poor relief. Married couples were split into separate buildings, their children sent to the workhouse school till they were nine, when they were sent away to be apprenticed. Paupers had to wear a special uniform, no possessions were allowed and compulsory prayers were said in the morning and evening.

***

Arthur Payne had decided it was time to put his proposal to his two young lodgers of the action that he thought they should now take. Rachel was in agreement that after several days of carpentry and procrastination, or in his own words, 'of joinery, cloud-watchin' an' moonin' abart all day', the apprentices had to return to their northern home. As far as Arthur could see things, if they sneaked back like fugitives then they risked arrest and serious criminal punishment.

Whereas, he reasoned, if they did things more openly and expressed a wish to return to their master to complete their apprenticeship, then they might still be able to see their mothers before leaving.

"They'd be officially escorted o' course—by someone in aufority, such as a constable or a bailiff. All depends on the beak—the magistrate, see."

"Better still, Arthur, if it were one o' the masters from the cotton mill, eh?"

"That's as maybe, Rachel. An' that's a long way orf yet, methinks. First, they gotter be talked into tellin' their story to the beak, an' then 'ope 'e shows 'em a bit o' consideration. They ain't all kind, an' unnerstandin' in my experience, gell."

"Oh, I remember some o' the stories ye told me, Art. But, I sees the sense o' what ye sayin'. No point settin' court fines to the lads, cus I reckon they ain't got much money between the pair on 'em."

That evening a serious discussion took place at the small dinner table in the Payne's living room. The topic of the conversation was gradually moved from the improved function of the old wooden door to the aims and promises that had been discussed several days earlier.

"Ye see, lads, if y'are going to become skilled workers in the way o' the cotton trade, then ye must return to the mill, where yer've come from. Did ye really mean what ye said?"

Thomas was first to reply.

"Oh, aye, Mr Payne. It's what I've learned summat about already. An' it ain't so bad I s'pose. A bit 'ard at times but we gets our food an' clothes while we're a learnin' the trade."

"An' we gets a bit o' learnin' about readin' an' writin' from Mrs Greg or one of 'er daughters. Though I'd like a lot more practice o' readin' proper," added Joseph.

Mrs Payne spoke at this point.

"I'm so pleased to hear ye say that, Joseph. Readin' and writin' proper are gonner be so important to yer future life, if ye really want to better yourselves."

"You ain't the first person to tell us that, Mrs Payne," said Joseph. "We both feel so beholdin' to you an' Mr Payne for all the trouble ye both 'ave gone to. Makin' us comfortable an' that. Ain't that right, Tommy?"

"It is. An' we truly respect all yer 'elpful words an' such. We reckon we'd 'ave us skulls cracked by footpads or constables by now if you 'adn't o' took us in," Thomas said.

"Well," growled Arthur, "I reckon ye could be right there, Tommy lad. There's some reg'lar rogues ararnd 'ere at times an' I knows most of 'em."

At this the boys looked a little shocked. They wondered what sort of background Mr Payne could have had to gain such experience. He continued, "It's time for a bit o' straight talkin', lads. If the two o' yer trusts us, like yer says ye do, then yer'll tell us the truth abart which cotton mill yer from… And…er'll take a bit more advice from me. So, what yer got to say to that then? Do yer trust us?"

Feeling tricked into revealing the location of the Greg's mill was hard to take at first but both boys knew that they owed the Paynes something more than just money. Their gratitude had to be shown in a way that truly demonstrated how fond they'd become of this genuinely honest and caring pair of respectable elder citizens. Respecting their wisdom and opinion by returning their honesty suddenly seemed an immediate way of doing just that.

"O' course we trust you, Mr Payne—an' you an' all, Mrs Payne. That's right ain't it, Tommy?"

"O' course it is. I wished I'd 'ad a Grandma an' Grandpa just like you," said Thomas. "Only, I never knowed any at all, see."

"Me neither... An' it's Mr Greg's Quarry Bank Mill, in Styal, over the River Bollin," said Joseph, sheepishly.

"In the countryside," added Thomas for good measure.

"Right," said Arthur brusquely. "That's a start I s'pose... An' I'd be right ter fink yer didn't get permission orf this Mr Greg to come darn 'ere to see yer muvvers, would'n I?"

"Steady, Art," interjected Rachel, dabbing at a few tears. "That would o' taken a lot out o' the boys to say. They've bin afeared of every shadder they've seen, an' every footstep they've 'eard for a week! Take a care, my dear."

With a softened tone Arthur continued, "Now then, lads, what we gotter be agreed on is 'ow best to do fings—so it don't make matters worse—for bofe yer muvvers. 'Specially arter yer've gorn back to that there Mr Greg's cotton mill... Am I right?"

Thomas held out his hand and spoke up first, "See, I lost a finger, Mr Payne, in the mill... 'An I wanted to see me ma—Oh, so much did I—but Mr Greg 'e said no, so I come to London anyway, 'an Joe said 'e would 'elp me find 'er, 'an all the way down 'ere I've been scared... 'An I'm still scared, but—I would so like to see me mother to tell 'er as 'ow I want to take care on 'er—'an any young'uns as well, like—so she don't need to worry no more... But—"

"Whoa, now, Tommy, Lad. Yer'd better slow darn an' take a breff afore ye swoons o' 'sphyxiation," replied Arthur with a chuckle in his voice.

"But you're right in sayin' all that about makin' sure we don't add any more ruin to us mother's lives, Mr Payne. I would o' come down any road. It weren't just to bring Tommy down wi' me, see... But we would both like it so much to see 'em, like; even just for a few minutes... It's the fear o' steppin' inside o' that workhouse. We just—"

"Aye, Joe, we understand We do, we really do," said Rachel taking each of their hands in hers and squeezing them as a gesture of her fondness. "And I think it's time, now there's a bond o' sorts betwixt us, that ye start to call us by our Christian names,

135

eh? Rachel an' Arthur. We'd take it very kindly if ye'd do that. Wouldn't we Art?" She sent a brief warning look at her husband not to disagree with her.

"Aye, that's right—amongst ourselves. But if we're in the presence of any officials, like a magistrate or a constable or a gen'leman, stick to Mr and Mrs, eh? So's they don't fink yer've got no respect. It'll 'elp a lot, see." Arthur added this last sentence with a wink and a conspiratorial tap to the side of his nose with his forefinger. The boys nodded.

"Right, nah then we're gettin' somewhere, llads. I'm keen to 'elp so ye must let me see a few people that might be able to smoove fings along so ter speak. But, for now, I need to 'ear ye promise me that ye will say all the good fings abart yer master an' 'is cotton mill when yer goes before the beak. Cus that's what will 'appen. Ye mark me words."

"Beak?" asked Joseph.

"The Magistrate," replied Arthur.

There was audible gulp from each apprentice that had much more to do with their apprehension than their supper.

"I wouldn't know what to say," said Thomas, looking helplessly at Rachel.

"Did yer master, Mr Greg, treat ye right, Tommy?" she asked.

"Oh, aye, he were all right wi' us, I suppose."

"Then that's what ye bofe must say," said Arthur. "That ye had no reason ter complain o' Mr Greg or any of 'is managers."

"They're called overlookers," said Joseph. "We could tell the magistrate about the food an' clothes we're given as well I s'pose... An' where we slept."

"There y'are," said Arthur. "That's jast the sort o' fing, I mean. Bein' 'appy wi' yer vittles is a right good fing to say ter 'is lordship, if y'ave to."

"Should I tell 'im as ow me finger got tore off in one o' the machines, Arthur?"

"I don't see no cause not to, Tommy."

"Ye might draw a bit o' sympaffy out o' the magistrate," said Rachel.

Arthur pulled a very doubtful face at this.

"Aye, ye might—but don't get yer 'opes up, Lad."

"What abart attendin' Church, Thomas? Did ye get a proper Christian education about the Lord thy Maker?"

"Oh, we did, Rachel, in Wilmslow. An' I've been tryin' to say me prayers reg'lar this past week."

She nodded with approval and looked at Joseph who said, "We 'ad to go twice to Church every Sunday, Rachel."

"Good," said Arthur. "Tomorrer, I'm gonner see some important people abart the situation wi' yer muvvers, an' maybe the little uns an all… See what I can get sorted, eh?"

The two boys nodded but doubt had already crept into Joseph's eyes. He was remembering the burly be-whiskered men that ran out of Hackney workhouse and chased them.

"Pardon me for asking, Arthur, but why're they goin' to listen to you? Them two constables that wanted to arrest us din't look the sort to listen to much reasonin'… An' with you sayin' as 'ow we can't make things worse for our mothers… Well… I'm a bit concerned, like."

Arthur stood up from the table and said, "Stay 'ere the bofe o' yer—an' don't move!"

Ten minutes later, he walked back into the living room and his appearance caused the boys to gasp with astonishment. He was wearing his watchman outfit, which included a heavy pitch black great cloak, that reached almost to the floor, a long wooden staff and a tall black hat, somewhat battered but adding even more height to the old man, who was now straight and proud. In his other hand, he carried a lantern and over his shoulder hanging from a leather strap was a large wooden rattle. Grinning at the effect he'd caused, he gave Joe his staff to hold and placed the lantern on the table. Pulling aside his cloak to reveal a long and shiny brass cutlass hanging from his belt,

Arthur then took hold of the handle of the rattle and turned to look at Rachel. When his grin widened even further she jumped up from the table and ran from the room, shouting, "Oh no! Oh no!" The door between the living room and the kitchen slammed shut. This was a signal for Arthur to take firm hold of the rattle's handle and give it a powerful swing. Round and round and round went the wooden clapper producing such an ear-splitting clattering, rattling sound that Thomas and Joseph had to cover their ears with their hands and plead: "Stop! Stop! Please, Arthur, stop! I can bear it no more."

He stopped, put down the rattle and held the cutlass aloft. "I was watchman around these parts for more 'an thirty year. Well known to constables an' thieves alike, an' one or two beaks, as well I might add. This 'ere blade served us bofe well in good King George's army. First me old dad, an' then me; an' then it's 'elped me arrest quite a few as watchman I can tell thee. They was soon persuaded ter accompany me darn to the Watch House for to occupy the prison cell there."

He sheathed the cutlass, shouldered the rattle and with the lantern in one hand and the staff in the other said, "Course I won't be needin' all this to visit the people I was talkin' abart but the cloak an' hat'll help 'em remember me—an' I reckon to give me the time I needs to ask a few favours on behalf o' thee."

The stunned apprentices remained subdued and quiet for the rest of the evening and each had a restless night's sleep. What would the next few days bring? It was a question they kept asking each other and one that ran through their minds in the darkness of the night.

***

Arthur Payne's first call the next day was to Hackney workhouse and he found the master there not as helpful as he had hoped. Mr Taylor seemed to be irritated by the situation.

"I don't see why you have these apprentices in your charge, Arthur, when the letter from Mr Greg was received by our Trustees. In fact, I have two bailiffs out looking for them this very moment, as they have been every day for almost a week now. The ruffians were seen and ran off."

He fiddled and fussed about with the papers on his desk.

"I have a note here to tell me about a warrant from a Justice of the Peace for Chester. It would appear that Mr Greg has informed the authorities there about their absconding." He continued to search through the papers, saying, "It must be here somewhere... I only had it a day ago."

"Well, ye see, Mr Taylor, I knows one o' the lads from when he was born. His muvver was a neighbour o' mine an' so I talked 'em into 'andin' themselves in an' goin' back to the cotton mill they run away from."

The master stopped fiddling with his papers, sat back in his chair and looked up at Arthur who was still standing.

"Oh, I see... Well, I don't actually... You're not here officially then. So why are dressed in your watchman uniform? I thought you'd retired years ago."

"I reckoned it'd 'elp me see one or two important people, like yerself, abart it. The beak maybe."

The master suspected that this statement of Arthur's was meant to flatter him and, in spite of himself, it worked. He seemed to grow larger and even more puffed up with importance.

"Hmm, it might get you into the Old Sessions, I suppose. And what do you want from me?"

"All these lads want is to see their muvvers, Mr Taylor. Mrs Priestley is still 'ere in the workhouse, I believe and... Mrs Sefton left to work in the kitchens o' one o' the big 'ouses over in Boe-voyer Tarn."

"De Beauvoir Town, eh? I don't remember where she went—and I don't have time to find out, Arthur—not at all. So please don't ask... Now, I'm very busy, so if you don't mind, I'll say goodbye to you."

"Course not, Mr Taylor; you're a busy man. But if I 'ad yer say so then I could 'ave a word wi' the lads ma, while I'm 'ere."

"And what good would that do, Arthur? Surely the main concern is to return the runaways back to their rightful master, Mr Samuel Greg."

"Well, ye see, Mr Taylor, by my ways o' finkin'—if the lads gets ter see their muvvers now they're darn 'ere, stands to reason they ain't gonner try an' run away agin, to see 'em agin later, see."

"Hmm, I can see some logic in what you say but there's no guarantee that this sort of person will not keep lying to you—and me and indeed, anyone else—just to get their way."

"Nah then, Mr Taylor, that's just where ye gotter trust me, see. Me an' the missus know'd Joe's ma from long ago, afore 'er usband, John, went orf for ter fight for king an' country. Bofe on 'em decent folks, none o' yer robbin' an' disreputable types, Mr Taylor, believe me. An' she come darn on 'er luck when 'e was a baby an' that's 'ow come she wound up in the workhouse, see."

"Hmm, and the boy? How does he strike you? How old is he now?"

"Oh, 'e must be 16 or 17 this year. Fine-lookin' lad now 'e is an' 'e wants ter pay 'is way. Bofe lads a' been 'elpin' me repair me frant door for a week, an' don't want naffin' for it, so they don't. Even gimmee the wood for the job an' don't spect no payment for it. Joe's a decent lad, Mr Taylor, an' no mistake. I respect 'is promises. Lay me repoo-tayshun on it."

"That says a lot, Arthur, since I can recall how well you carried out your very difficult duties in the past... Take a seat and let me think on what you have said while I just have a word with the matron, my wife."

So, saying the Master of Hackney workhouse left the room.

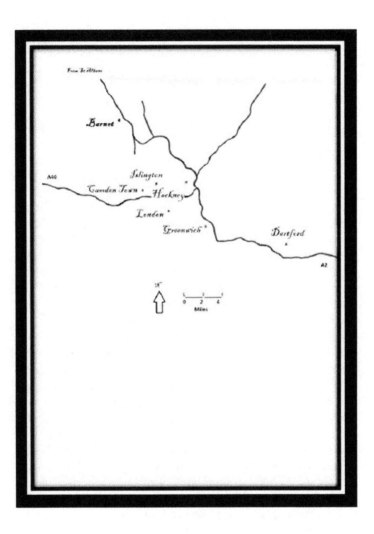

From St Albans

Barnet

A40

Islington

Camden Town

Hackney

London

Greenwich

Dartford

A2

N

0   2   4
Miles

141

Chapter 11
Maximillian Leodet

Arthur Payne was allowed to speak for a few minutes to Catherine Priestley, Thomas' mother, in the master's office and in the presence of Mr and Mrs Taylor. He had agreed to certain conditions laid out before him by the master. Chief amongst these was his agreement to carry a letter, written there and then by the master and addressed to a certain Mr Leodet, a local magistrate of the acquaintance of both men. After his conversation with Mrs Priestley, he had to next visit the Old Sessions and seek an audience with this same 'beak'.

Mrs Priestley was a shrivelled sparrow of a woman whose wan appearance gave Arthur great concern, for Tommy's future peace of mind, if they were ever to meet; moreover he doubted his mother's future ability to survive many more years in the workhouse. Her seven years working as a drudge and a skivvy in the kitchens and the wash house had taken their toll upon her health. She told Arthur that had it not been for her wish to see Thomas again and the occasional glimpse of her 'babbies' in the infants' quarters, she'd have died years earlier. This remark caused grave and disappointing looks from the master and the matron but Catherine Priestley had long ago ceased trying to win favours from either. The plump and jolly stature of the married couple belied their sour and disagreeable features, with frequent cruel comments directed at the inmates.

She wept continuously when she heard that Thomas had risked the long journey to London in order to see her. Frail murmurings of, "Oh, Tommy, my Tommy," between her sobs interjected any discussion elsewhere in the room. Her pleas to be given permission to see him were met with the reminder from the master that the inmates of the workhouse were not prisoners.

"If you wish to seek absence, Catherine, you merely have to give me three hours' notice, the same as any other inmate."

"An' the children?" asked Arthur.

"As you well know, Arthur, they became the responsibility of the workhouse when their mother was accepted as a pauper of the workhouse, needing poor relief. Their future will be decided at the appropriate time by their superiors."

Arthur wondered whether he should ask his next question, not wishing to upset the poor sobbing woman who had collapsed in his vacant chair, at the first mention of Thomas. He decided she should know the answer and spoke.

"If Mrs Priestley gives this three hours' notice ye speak of, Mr Taylor, does it mean she 'as to apply again for poor relief?"

"That would be the case in my opinion. So, it is an action that requires careful consideration."

"Yes, indeed," opined Mrs Taylor, not wishing to be left out of the conversation. She sniffed in a disapproving manner and folded her arms across her chest, as if to send a message that she had much better things to do than argue with a pauper.

"An' is it not in yer powers to grant the poor woman a short leave to see 'er son? The lad ain't seen 'is ma for nigh on five years, I believe."

"That's as maybe, Mr Payne, but I don't make the rules. The Trustees would need to have a meeting about this."

An hour later, Arthur was sat in the corridors of the Middlesex Sessions House awaiting an audience with Mr Leodet who was in his courtroom. It was a busy day in the rooms of litigation and justification of British law and it meant Arthur was sat for two more hours before he saw the magistrate. Mr Leodet, a tall, balding man with an intimidatingly large nose, recognised Arthur as he swept imperiously down the corridor.

"Ah, Mr Payne, I am informed by my clerk, Mr Gardilly, that you are in possession of a missive from the Master of Hackney workhouse. Can this be true?"

His piercing, grey eyes and black beetling brows immediately reminded Arthur of the magistrate's innate ability to extract, in varying degrees, tears and confessions from the prisoners in his courtroom.

"Aye, Mr Leodet, an' 'ere it is. An' I'd be grateful for the opportoonity ter discuss the contents o' this 'ere letter wi' ye. If ye 'ave the place an' time for such as meself."

"I remember you well, Mr Payne, and a more diligent and honest servant of the Crown it would be hard to find than yourself. Follow me, Sir."

So, saying, the magistrate led Arthur up two short flights of highly polished stairs and into a large room with oak-panelled walls that he shared with two other colleagues.

"Aha, I see my fellow magistrates are occupied elsewhere, so if it is a matter of some delicacy, requiring a little privacy, then we may speak here. The ante-rooms are a little cramped at this time with a great number of new documents for our perusal. Sit you down, Mr Payne."

Arthur sat down in a well-worn Windsor chair at the enormous wooden desk that Mr Leodet indicated with a sweep of his arm. He found a place beneath his chair for his battered black hat. Before him there were piles of documents across the top of the desk and others littering the floor on either side of it. After listening to Arthur and reading the letter, the magistrate took out, from one of the locked desk drawers, a bottle of port and poured them both a small glass.

"Just a little lubrication, to help the talking tackle in our throats. I daresay you'd appreciate it at this point in a busy day, like I do myself, Mr Payne?"

Since it was Arthur's first experience of such hospitality from a magistrate, he nodded in agreement and they clinked glasses. The warm glow that hit his chest and flowed slowly upwards to his throat caused him to comment:

"Hmm, very nice, if I may say so, Mr Leodet. An' what, er… I mean ter say… Do ye… Erm—"

"Yes, what of the letter, Mr Payne, or will you let me call you Arthur? After all, it was over many years we had cause to meet and discuss some of the many law breakers you brought before the courts in this—and the old—building. Thus, now you are retired according to Mr Taylor," He held the letter aloft. "I would like to think of you as an old friend—first name terms. What do you think?"

Arthur was so taken aback at this that he said nothing, his lower jaw slowly sagged down until Mr Leodet had to add:

"Hmm, I see you are shocked by my request. Well, no matter. When you are ready; my unfortunate Christian name is Maximillian, Max for short, and I will address you as—"

"Arthur is fine, Sir. An' if ye don't mind, I'll feel a lot more comfortable sticking to Mr Leodet for the time being?"

"No matter, as I say. The reason for my apparent break with the conventions and niceties of our—Status quo, shall I say?—is because you are here dressed in your old 'official' uniform to request something which, in all honesty, we have to agree is not 'official', not authorised by the law—other than your bounden duty as an honest citizen. Am I right?"

"I 'spose so, Mr Leodet."

Suddenly, Arthur felt exposed and vulnerable, unable to think straight. What had he led himself into? Was the law about to accuse him of something?

"Quite so, quite so, Arthur. Correct me if I am wrong but it is my belief that what you wish is," he paused to add effect to his next few words, "a favour. You require a favour, such as is often asked of a friend. So, since, as Mr Taylor cares to point out, the two boys have absconded from their apprentice master and broken the terms of their indenture, which as we both know is against the law, then that is the most significant legal matter we must deal with. Without any further delay, I might add. But a favour between friends requires a conversation on first name terms. What do you say now—Arthur?"

Arthur chuckled, recognising that he had been out-manoeuvred. He held out his half-empty glass and said, "I'd like another drop o' that fine port, if yer've a mind, Max? And I've a favour to request from ye, if yer've time to listen?"

His new friend smiled, topped up Arthur's glass and said, "I'd be mightily grateful, Arthur, if you'd explain just why you feel justified in taking these two runaways under your wing and daring to come to me with such a request?"

"Ye see, Max," he paused, to get used to the sound of his own voice mouthing that word, drank a little more and continued, "I spent nigh on thirty year arrestin' folk, an' bringin' 'em to court to face the consequences o' their criminality. An' I knowed, all along o' them thirty years that some o' those people, men, women an' kids ain't never 'ad a chance, a proper chance ter get a foot up any kind o' ladder for a better life. But I knew

145

me dooty an' got 'em locked up to face the courts an' be punished."

Arthur waited for Max to respond, wondering whether he should continue. Max responded with a curious smile and a gentle wave of his right hand.

"Nah then, ye see, Mr… Erm… Max, we've got two lads 'ere who want to do the right thing by their muvvers. An' their only crime is runnin' away, when they was distressed, ter see 'em. But they've agreed to go back an' learn their trade so's they can support the family arterwards. We give 'em a chance to see their kin an' they'll do the right fing. I knows it in me bones, Max. Punish 'em, by denyin' 'em the chance to see their muvvers an' they might become yer real criminals out o' regret an' bitterness, see."

The magistrate sipped more port then, thoughtfully, tapped his lips with a forefinger.

"You have made your thoughts and wishes clear, Arthur. Would that some of the representatives I see in my court could speak so clearly. If I can help these young men meet their mothers before they return to their apprentice master, who according to this letter is a Mr Samuel Greg, then I have a proposition to put to you. Will you now hear me out?"

Arthur finished his drink, sat back in his chair and listened to Maximillian Leodet with some apprehension.

***

When Arthur finally arrived back home, it was too late in the evening to carry out the third of the tasks that he had set for himself early that morning when leaving Frog Lane. Through his conversation with Thomas' mother, he had discovered which of the large houses in De Beauvoir Town, was the place of employment for Joseph's mother. Both boys were naturally very excited to hear all of this news and he had to first assure Thomas about his ma's health and then tell Joseph there was a chance that he could be seeing Mrs Sefton the very next day. It had been a tiring day for the old man and he wanted to retire to his bed after supper but gave the boys a few more minutes for their questions before doing so.

"Yes, Joe, I will be goin' up to Boe-voyer Tarn but I ain't too sure if it's a good idea for ye to accompany me, see."

He waved two sealed letters at them and continued, "It's all in these letters. Ye see, the magistrate I spoke to today, he laid darn some conditions ye bofe gotter stick to, see. An' one or two more terms, for meself."

"Oh, Arthur, my dear, what 'ave ye agreed to? I 'ope you two boys appreciates all o' the trouble 'e's gorn to for the pair o' thee. No doubt risked 'is good name an' everythin'.'."

"Oh, Mrs Payne… Rachel," said Joseph. "We ain't about to put you nor Arthur to no more trouble. On my life, on my ma's life, I promise you, we will do whatever Arthur asks. If only we could just see our mothers for ten minutes and put their minds at rest… Then we both agree to go back to Mr Greg's mill an' finish our apprenticeships. Soon as you like. I'm right, ain't I, Tommy? You think just the same."

"I promise everythin' Joe's just spoke of, Rachel. On my life. We just want to see our mothers more than anything in the world."

"Right y'are, boys. An' what o' the little 'uns, Art? Did ye get to see 'em?"

"Nah, Rachel, I didn't. The master wasn't too keen on lettin' me much further into the workhouse than 'is rooms. But yer ma told me their names, Tommy. The boy is called Eddy, arter yer ma's father, Edward; an' the little gal's named Lizzy, arter-"

"After me grandma," interrupted Thomas. "Mother's ma was called Elizabeth, I remember. But I never saw 'er…"

"An' the Matron was at pains ter tell me that they're doing pretty well. Just like Daniel, yer little bruvver, Joe."

"Well, that's good to hear ain't it, boys?" said Rachel.

"Will we ever see 'em, Arthur?" asked Thomas.

"I ain't gonner lie to yer, lads. The master an' 'is missus, the matron, were none too keen at all on that subject; but the magistrate's written a request to 'em abart it, so we'll 'ave ter see, eh. Same as getting' yer ma 'is permission to wave ye goodbye—on Saturday."

This was a surprising revelation to the apprentices.

"Saturday! Why, what's to happen on Saturday, Arthur?" asked Joseph.

147

"That's August the second, Joe. The date the magistrate 'as set aside for the two o' yer to appear afore 'im to explain yerselves. Runnin' away from the mill an' such."

"What's today?" asked Joseph.

"Why, bless ye, Lad, it's Thursday, July the thirty first," answered Rachel. "An' I think that's enough questions for now. We're all tired—but specially my old man, ere. 'E's got a lot more walkin' on yer behalf tomorrer, Joseph."

The boys each stuck out a manly hand in an effort to shake Arthur's hand to show their gratitude.

"We won't let you down, Arthur," said Joseph.

The old man shook hands with both, saying, "Don't 'spect ye'll be shut o' me yet, lads. I've promised to escort ye to court an' then all the way back to Cheshire if they can't get anyone else afore Saturday."

Rachel sighed, shook her head in surrender at this news but said nothing except, "Nah get orf up the wooden hill, the three o' yer. Get some shuteye. Yer gonner need it I've no doubt."

A few minutes later, Joseph joined Thomas kneeling in prayer beside their bed. All of their hopes for things to go well were now in God's hands and he reasoned that an earnest plea to the Lord could do no harm. Then they each added a thankful prayer for Rachel and Arthur, while they were on their knees, stomachs churning in anticipation of what the next two days may bring.

Chapter 12
Middlesex to Cheshire

"Why ye 'ad to say ye'd take the boys all o' that way back to Cheshire is beyond me, Art. I knows we're fond of 'em but ye only ever done escortin' on a journey a few times, an' it were a tirin' task, as I remember. An' ye were a lot younger an' it wasn't so far away, as I recall."

It was very early on Friday and Arthur was preparing to walk to De Beauvoir Town with the letter for Esther Sefton's employer. From there, he would walk to deliver the other letter from Mr Leodet to the Master of Hackney workhouse. He knew that the magistrate had worded both letters to sound as though the case before him might require the presence of each mother as a witness. Both men had agreed that this should be sufficient cause for them to be given a few hours leave. Arthur had not mentioned this previously in case the fates should dash the boy's high hopes to the ground.

"Oh, I'll be all right, gell. I knows I'm a bit creaky wi' the rheumatiz at times but once I gets agoin' I'm fine. An' any way it ain't certain it'll be me as goes. There's a couple o' bailiffs an' constables could go instead o' me. An' this 'ere Mr Greg might send darn one of 'is own men to take the lads back."

Rachel scoffed at this, "An' pigs might fly, Art. If them officials can save a bit o' cash we bofe know they will. There ain't no time to send letters orf to the boys' master. I knows that. If there's reliable old Arthur Payne awillin' ter do it, then that'll do. I ain't such an old fool as me old man is but—"

She raised a hand to stop Arthur's further objections.

"But, old man, I've grown very fond o' them two lads an' if there's anybody on this God's Earth that I'd trust ter take good care on 'em all that way—then it's you, yer old fool." She patted his cheek gently and added, "So ye takes good care o' yerself, as well. Nah we got that little bit o' pension I'd like ter spend a few more years enjoyin' it wi' ye."

Arthur leant down and kissed his wife gently.

"I'll be all right, gell. I've got me books an' yer've got yer sewin', an' it's not so bad is it, this 'ere retirin' time o' life. So, I'll be back ter share it together wi' ye, afore ye knows it."

Before he set off, Arthur and Rachel had to spend some time resisting Joseph's pleas to accompany him to De Beauvoir Town. They argued that, although they understood how much he longed to see his mother again, it was very likely Mrs Sefton would become so emotional when reunited with her son that it might affect her work for the rest of the day. If her employer was not of the understanding sort then his mother could be out of a job again and back in the workhouse before he'd even reached Quarry Bank Mill. Despite his brave efforts to hold back his tears, Joseph had to endure many hours on that Friday weeping with an aching heart, but at least he had a comforting friend's arm around his shoulders.

Arthur returned to Frog Lane in the afternoon, an hour earlier this time, still weary but feeling a little more positive than the previous day. His reception at 'the big house' in De Beauvoir Town was not cordial at first. Although the number of servants there was not big, the butler took his duties very seriously and insisted that Arthur wait inside the servants' entrance, at the rear of the building. He was not impressed at all by the watchman's uniform and inspected the magistrate's seal on the letter most closely before taking it to the lady of the house.

"Mr Critchmole is on important business in town. I will see whether Mrs Critchmole has time to see you."

While waiting there, a young woman passed him by with a bowl of something that breathed out steam, from beneath its lid. She paused, frowning, trying to recall the watchman's face to memory. "Is it Arthur Payne?"

"Aye, Esther, it is. An' I must say as 'ow ye're lookin' very well. Are fings agoin' well for ye?"

She glanced about her to check that no-one could see them or was within earshot.

"Yes, thank you for askin', Arthur. Have ye brought word o' Daniel? Only I was worried about 'is teacher in Hackney. She's greatly addicted to the taste o' gin an' swears too much, an' not too keen on soap an' water to my way o' thinkin'. Why she's there I—"

"Hush! I'll tell thee more later, Esther. I can hear footsteps on them stairs."

The kitchen maid hurried away to the scullery and closed the door as the butler arrived.

"Follow me," he ordered. "Mrs Critchmole will see you in the sitting room."

The lady of the house was most concerned, initially, that Esther was not in any kind of trouble and so Arthur was able to reassure her that the court case could not possibly bring a stain on the household, or upon Esther's good character. He delicately reminded Mrs Critchmole of the great opportunity she had given Esther to gain employment and take her leave of the workhouse.

"It is to be 'oped, ma'am, that more folks, such as yerself, could do such good Christian deeds for them poor women who's darn on their luck in Hackney workhouse, eh?"

"Perhaps you are right, Mr Payne. Cook and I have been most satisfied with Esther. She is diligent and has fitted in well. We would hate to lose her. What is it she is to be witness to?"

"Ye'll 'ave to forgive me if I ain't at liberty to answer that question directly, Ma'am. I'd be in trouble wi' the magistrate, see. Seein' as 'ow I'm 'ere as a servant o' the court, so ter speak."

"Of course, of course, Mr Payne. Forgive me for asking."

"No matter, Ma'am... Ye may recall as 'ow Mrs Sefton got darn on 'er luck when 'er 'usband went orf ter fight in the war wi' the French?"

Mrs Critchmole nodded. "So, I was told."

"Right, well, their son, Joseph, was later apprenticed to a cotton mill. Way up norf it were, in Cheshire, see."

"That much I also know, Mr Payne."

"Right, well then, Mrs Critchmole, not ter waste no more o' yer time. The nit an' grit o' the matter is young Joseph an' 'is friend, Thomas, 'ave come darn ter London, 'opin' ter see their muvvers. Broke their indentures, see. So, nah, they're in court tomorrer an' their muvvers is called as witnesses."

"I see, so Esther will need some time off... Tomorrow is Saturday and we have nothing in particular planned that requires

151

her presence. I cannot see that being a problem and I'm sure that Mr Critchmole will agree with me."

"Thank ye, Ma'am. If ye could just remind 'er tomorrer, abart the time she must be there."

"It says in this letter ten o'clock, so if she leaves no later than nine; the Old Assizes are less than two miles from here and that will give her plenty of time, I think. Do you need to speak to her, Mr Payne?"

"A quick word would be appreciated, Ma'am. An' I must thank ye so kindly for yer 'elp in the matter."

Mrs Critchmole vacated the room after sending for Esther which gave Arthur time to explain things about Joseph. He was at pains to assure her that nothing had been said about Daniel. The Paynes knew he had been conceived in the workhouse and the father, described by Rachel as a 'drunken ne'er-do-well', had later been found drowned in the Thames. Esther had been close to swooning in front of Arthur on hearing that Joseph was living with the Paynes. With a little rest in a sitting room chair and a drink of cold water, she had recovered enough to assure him that she would be there the next day. Arthur then went on to Hackney workhouse to deliver Mr Taylor's letter and, although the master thought it 'most likely' that Thomas' mother would be in the courthouse for ten o'clock, he refused to say anything about the three children: Daniel, Lizzy and Eddy.

On his journey home, Arthur was full of regrets and self-recrimination for not allowing either of the apprentices to accompany him to the Critchmole's house or to the workhouse. The reception at the former residence went much better than he'd anticipated and he observed that the Hackney Master had strong doubts about refusing to grant the magistrate's written wishes. So, their mothers could have spent more time with the sons they had not seen for many years; and he felt a strong uncertainty about the time that they would be allowed together in court the next day. The one thing that Maximillian Leodet had been most insistent about was that the apprentices would be returned to Quarry Bank Mill immediately after he had heard each of them 'speak their piece in court'. The travel arrangements for their return were being made as Arthur went about his journey and a bill for their cost, made out to Mr Greg, would be carried by the officer of the court who would accompany the apprentices.

Thomas and Joseph had legs of jelly as they approached the Middlesex Sessions House before nine on Saturday morning. As if the occasion was not frightening enough, there was a gigantic mountain of a buildings facing them, daring them to enter, and challenging them to speak against the laws of the land. Both boys would have turned and fled all the way back to Styal had Arthur not been with them, encouraging them to speak the truth—but advising them about one or two points that may not go down too well with 'his worship'. So, he told them a little bit of paraphrasing may need to be used when answering questions, though he used the words 'tweakin' 'ere an' there'.

The boys were to be questioned one after the other and when Joseph entered the court, he faced a panel of three Justices of the Peace, Mr Leodet in the centre, as the chairman. His colleagues looked a great deal older than the chairman with their long grey hair around a monkish pate and deep-set, expressionless, watery eyes in dark sockets. Arthur was disappointed to find that neither of the boys' mothers was present to watch the proceedings, and therefore provide the moral support he'd hoped would bolster their courage.

Joseph nervously confirmed his name, age, place of birth and parental roots as best he could. He agreed to the details about his apprenticeship to Samuel Greg's mill and then, remembering Arthur's advice, proceeded to praise the working and living conditions of the apprentices there, going into some detail. He made a point of including the words, 'I liked my employment very well' and later, 'I have no reason to complain of my master Mr Greg nor Richard Bamford who overlooked the workers there… ' Joseph described the sleeping arrangements in the Apprentice House, how well they were fed and how often they attended church on Sundays.

Later, he confirmed that he and Thomas had left, without the permission of Mr Greg, to walk most of the way to London in order to see their mothers. When asked about where they found the money for food and so on, during the journey, he took care not to mention selling wooden products. Arthur had told the boys that without a pedlar's licence, they could later face more serious charges, so Joe said that they had helped herd cattle for wages when his own money, for working overtime at the mill, ran out. He was sure that they did not need to spend more than two or three pence a day having slept free sometimes in farm buildings or with friends. Having almost come to the end of his statement, Joseph was beginning to feel angry and abandoned because each time he looked around the court for sight of his mother there was none. Even Arthur Payne had left the courtroom.

What is to happen to me now? he thought as the clerk witnessed his signature and a bailiff led him to an ante-room, to await the magistrates' decision following Thomas' appearance.

Feeling as if he would vomit with fear at every question, Thomas confirmed similar details about his background before arriving at the mill. Then Thomas was not able to reveal as much detail about the conditions for the apprentices as Joseph, so obviously afraid was he. The panel of JPs had agreed to be more considerate towards Thomas in view of his young age. He did his best to describe his work and how he had lost a finger but took care to say he recovered because of Dr Holland's attentions. Thomas' most frightening moment came when asked where he had found the money for everything on their journey. He looked around the courtroom: Where was his mother? She should be present so he had been told. He immediately forgot all they had agreed about selling wood or herding cattle and blurted out to their worships that his mother had sent him a crown of five shillings.

However, thinking hard, he could remember two sentences he had practised with Joseph and said, "I have no reason to complain of the usage I received during this time…" And after confirming they had walked nearly all the way, stopped with friends and spent thrupence a day, he carefully added, "I am very willing to go back again."

Both statements having been witnessed by Mr Leodet's clerk, Mr Samuel Gardilly, the two apprentices waited together in the ante-room in the presence of a bailiff who sported orange mutton chop whiskers.

When he had realised that neither of the apprentices' mothers were present in the courtroom, Arthur had slipped out to find out more. Huddled together, sat weeping and distraught, Esther and Catherine looked up to see him approach.

"Why are ye here, ladies?" he asked. "Ye should be in there wi' ye sons. They need yer presence in court."

"When we got 'ere, Mr Payne, an' spoke together, we grew so upset an' nervous that we thought it best not to go in," said Catherine, suddenly becoming a small tower of strength. "We felt it might go harder for 'em, if their mothers are makin' a fuss."

"An' then, when we decided to go in after all, the feller over there wouldn't let us in," added Esther.

Arthur looked at the usher guarding the door, who knew they were talking about him, and he returned his look with a stern shake of the head. Arthur turned back to the women with eyebrows raised in confusion.

"He told us we were still blubbing too much and would cause a distraction… And…"

"An' what, Catherine?"

"An' I swore at 'im for being such an awkward cuss," she answered.

"Well that, my dear, wouldna 'elped at all."

He sighed and explained. "When the lads come art o' court I expect 'em to get on some wagon or cart wi' me an' the driver. Then orf we goes to Cheshire, 'undreds o' miles away. That's me job for a day or two. I agreed it, otherwise ye would not a' been told to get time orf to be 'ere. If I don't take 'em then I'm gonner be in big trouble wi' 'is worship… Understand?"

They nodded and sniffed, dabbing away more tears with a corner of their shawls.

"What I fink ye should do is say yer goodbyes, an' all that, to yer boys as soon as they comes art o' that side room. Cus I can't gi' yer more 'an a few minutes, see. I've got all o' their stuff wi' mine, all ready ter go. It's bin all arranged, see. Them's the terms I 'ad to say yes to."

The women hugged each other and Arthur could see there were no little children with them, so thought it better not to bring up the subject. He decided that Hackney workhouse's Master and Matron were still not quite as Christian, in their outlook towards those less fortunate than themselves, as they often pretended. A small fuss around the side door he had indicated caused both women to rush to it. The usher stepped back and out stepped Thomas and Joseph.

Amidst the hugging and weeping, kissing and promising, there stepped a burly man, whose bald head brought to one's mind a hard-boiled egg, but with a trace of bushy yolk on the

155

outside. He was attempting to extricate each of the apprentices from their mother and drag them out to the waiting wagon. The emotional huddle of four people was not about to give him the time of day, let alone any hint of co-operation to allow him to carry out what he saw as his 'duty as a bailiff'. A few squeals from the women and shouts from the young men worried the watching old watchman.

Arthur Payne stepped up to the crowd and spoke to the bailiff whose name he'd recalled, "Eh up, Bull, what yer abart? There's no need fer any o' that strong arm stuff."

"It's all right, Arthur, Mate, I'm just gonner bring 'em art to yer wagon. Ye can just wait art there wi' the driver. Gi' us a minute, eh?"

"Ye ain't listenin' to me, Bull. Stop all o' that pullin' and pushin' an' go an' 'ave yerself a cuppa rosey lee, will yer? I'm in charge on' 'em all nah, an' I've agreed it wi' 'is worship, see. Ten minutes wi' their family."

But Bull was not about to give way to Arthur and ignored him. Joseph's tear-filled eyes were turning red with rage and he suddenly gave the big man a terrific shove in his mid-riff with all his might, which winded him. Arthur quickly stepped in between the two and told Joseph to wait outside with his mother who saw the sense of it. She hustled Joseph outside and Thomas and his mother followed them. The panting bailiff stared with malevolent eyes at Arthur and said, "Right… old man… yer a witness… to that assault on… a court officer… I want 'im back 'ere… Now! I'm gonner arrest 'im!"

"Nah, you ain't, Bull. Ye go an' calm darn wi' a cuppa like I said. An' we'll be orf to Cheshire like I bin ordered."

"Nah, nah, Arthur. I wants the lad in custody for assaultin' me. If yer don't go an' get 'im I will." He made a move towards the door prompting Arthur to put out his arm.

"Bull, Mate, don't do that. Yer causin' a delay ter me written orders from Max—an' that could get yer into a whole heap o' new trouble. I ain't forgot yer bit o' bovver in the past wi' bashin' too many skulls when it weren't needed."

"What you on abart? That all got sorted—sort of. Anyway, Arthur, you ain't even official no more. Yer retired."

"That's what I'm tryin' to tell ye, see. I'm specially appointed, by Max, ter this job o' taking the lads back to their

156

master in Cheshire. Gotter be immediately arter they bin examined in 'is courtroom—afore noon. If Max hears abart all this delay, well… Just let me get orf will ye?"

"Make sense will ye, Arthur! Who's this Max?"

At this, Arthur stepped back a little from Bull, raised his eyebrows in surprise and, just as he opened his mouth to reply, the enormous clock on the outside of the assizes building began to chime. The men counted and on the twelfth ring Arthur said, "Oh, my Lord, it's noon already. I gotter be orf, Bull. Max is probably still in 'is courtroom if ye need to check wi' 'im."

"Max who?"

"Max! Maximillian Leodet, the bloomin' magistrate. Who d'yer fink? We've become good friends since I retired, Bull… See ye, Mate."

Arthur hurried away and Bull thought about things for a few seconds, then he went away to make himself a cup of strong sweet tea. Outside, the two apprentices and their mothers had naturally taken advantage of the few extra minutes to reacquaint themselves. The little snippets of news they'd exchanged together would never be forgotten. When Arthur ordered the boys to assist him load up the wagon, they did so almost willingly, encouraged by the women, none wanting to disappoint the old man. Each son was shouting, earnestly repeating his promises as the wagon rolled away.

It gathered speed and the huddled pair of weeping, waving mothers grew smaller and smaller in the distance. Both runaways felt grateful to the Lord for the precious seconds they'd had to embrace their mothers once more. Desperately swallowing their grief at the parting, they continued to yell and shout, louder and louder with every few yards, with every anxious utterance.

Joe called out, "When I'm earning enough, I'm going to buy me a farm an' settle down an' get married—an' then you an' Daniel can come an' live with us, Ma. Her name's Ellie an' she's an artist—an' she's beautiful—just like you, Ma."

Unable to hold back his tears, Tommy's broken voice was almost lost on the wind with his last assurance, "I'm going to learn me all about the cotton trade, Ma, an' to learn to read an' write—so's I can send you letters. Then I can tell you when I'm comin' back 'ome again, to keep you an' Lizzy an' Eddy safe in our old house. We won't have any debts ever again, Ma."

The mothers started forward suddenly when the wagon reached a bend in the road, in a hopeless attempt to catch it up. And then it was gone, lost to sight, heading for the same drovers road, the Roman Road, which would take them back to Quarry Bank Mill in Styal, Cheshire.

Epilogue

One of Samuel Greg's major problems when establishing his mill beside the River Bollin in Styal was finding enough workers. The rapidly growing population of the nearest large town, Manchester, was still too far away at eleven miles for he needed his workers to attend regularly and punctually. Despite the growing improvements in the roads there was no reliable and efficient means of public transport available for the numbers of people that he required. The few villages nearby were very small and certainly had too few agricultural workers prepared to change their life style from one where they laboured on the land to one inside a mill, subject to bells that determined their working hours. Thus, like a few other mill owners of the time, Greg took advantage of the system that became known as pauper apprentices.

During the time of Thomas Priestley and Joseph Sefton Quarry Bank Mill was expanding steadily. Much later in the 19th century several of his sons would be involved in the management of the Greg's cotton empire. Under the stewardship of Robert Hyde Greg it would eventually grow to include mills in nearby Bollington, Reddish and Bury with others at Calver in Derbyshire and Caton near Lancaster. The building of an apprentice house, just a few hundred metres away from the mill, enabled as many as ninety children workers, from the approximate age of nine to their late teens, to be available. This supplemented up to half of the mill's total workforce at various times. It was not until much later in that century that Robert decided to close down the Quarry Bank Apprentice House as being uneconomical. But before that era hundreds of workhouse children from the parishes of Wilmslow, Newcastle-under-Lyme, Liverpool and London, amongst others, had been transported to Styal in closed wagons over the intervening years. While the mill owners, like the Gregs, provided clothing and so on for their child apprentices their business would receive cash payments from the parishes concerned for each workhouse child. The cost of providing for the poor had become such a very great drain upon local parishes that they were almost queueing up to send pauper children to factories and mills.

Of course using small children to complete menial tasks that 'earned their keep' was not something new for the 18th and 19th centuries. So called cottage industries would not have survived in most cases if the children of the family had not taken on some of the many jobs, both inside the home and outside on the land. Children were often indentured as apprentices as young as seven and bound to a 'master' as far back as Tudor times when many parents, no doubt, hoped to find a decent and reliably qualified master. Statutes of the time required anyone who practised a trade to have undergone a certain number of years training with a qualified master. Academic education of any worthwhile nature was always something for the better off sections of society and would continue to be so well into the later years of the Industrial Revolution. In the centuries before industrialisation the children of poor and working-class families had always laboured, helping around the house or helping in the family's various economic enterprises. Carding raw cotton or wool and spinning yarn were two of the most common tasks taken on by the children of families connected to the production of textiles before industrialization.

The general story of the children, who were 'apprenticed' to work in factories and mills, during the Industrial Revolution, is doubtless one of great unhappiness. When many of the children were as young as seven and working twelve, or more, hours a day for six days a week, then how can any modern person view such a situation with anything other than horror? However, there are several examples of employers and organisations who took their responsibilities towards their employees very seriously; such as, famously and later in the 19th century, the Lever Brothers, the Cadbury family and the Rowntrees; plus at this book's earlier time, Robert Owen. The Gregs, together with the Arkwrights and Samuel Oldknow, can also be included in this group of more enlightened employers within the textile industry.

That is not to say that working conditions within the factories and mills improved to such an extent that workers were generally made 'happier'. Robert Blincoe and others, including Samuel Greg, had an opportunity in 1833 to tell their stories about the working conditions, accidents and discipline seen there from their own point of view. The Commission for Inquiring into the Employment of Children in Factories was convened in April of 1833, when four teams of two civil servants and a physician were sent to the industrial centres of Britain. The results of their enquiries were collated in London by the Central Board whose primary purpose was to search for reforms that would contribute to the nation's wealth and happiness. Some examples of the statements made to the Factory Commission may give the reader a sense of just how quickly, or otherwise, things were to improve for workers, both younger and older.

Robert Blincoe, speaking about Litton Mill in Derbyshire:
"In the first place, they are standing upon one leg, lifting up one knee, a great part of the day, keeping the ends up from the spindle; I consider that that employment makes many cripples; then there is the heat and the dust: then there are so many different forms of cruelty used upon them, then they are so liable to have their fingers catched and to suffer other accidents from the machinery; then the hours is so long, that I have seen them tumble down asleep among the straps and machinery, and so get cruelly hurt..."

An account given by William Pickles, a boy from Ward's Mill in Bradford:
"My legs are now bent as you see... Got my knees bent with standing so long. Remember when my knees began to fail me; I had been at the mill not two years... my knees hurt me very bad then; when we're tired, you know, there was nought to sit on; I was obliged to lay hold of summat to keep me up... It used to be very bad towards night; sometimes very sleepy; we used to get thumped sometimes by the overlooker, who was a woman..."
It was noted by the commissioner: The knees are bent dreadfully, both inwards and forwards. The height of the boy, who is fifteen, is three feet nine inches (1.14 metre).

Here is some of Samuel Greg's evidence when answering the factory commissioner's questions:

Q: Is there any distinct or specific provision for the ventilation of your factory, if there is any such provision, describe its nature and effects?

A: "In scotching (cleaning the cotton) the dust and flock is carried off through flues by means of powerful fans, leaving the room perfectly free from inconvenience."

Q: State whether the provision depends on the opening of windows, or other casual means?

A: "Yes, every window opening at the top."

Q: Is the ventilation regulated by the foremen, or overlooker or manufacturer, or is it controlled at the discretion of all, or any of the persons employed?

A: "By the overlooker."

When asked by Dr Hawkins, a commissioner, about the 'forms of cruelty' used with the children, Robert Blincoe had no trouble recalling to memory some of his own experiences:

"I have seen the time when two hand-vices of a pound weight each, more or less, have been screwed to my ears… Then three or four of us have been hung at once on a cross beam above the machinery, hanging by our hands, without shirts or stockings… we used to stand up, in a skip, without our shirts, and be beat with straps or sticks; the skip was to prevent us from running away from the strap… they used to tie on a twenty-eight pounds weight (one or two at once), according to our size, to hang down on our backs, with no shirts on. I have had them myself. Then they used to tie one leg up to a faller, whilst the hands were tied behind."

There was a follow-up question from Hawkins to Blincoe:

"Did the masters know of these things, or were they done only by the overlookers?" to which he received the reply:

"The masters have often seen them, and have been assistants in them."

Provision of bed, board, clothing and even the basic elements of an education was not common amongst mill owners but some, such as those listed above, felt it was their moral duty to do so. Many of the boys employed by the Gregs rose to become overseers and clerks with several achieving positions at the level of management. For example, in the 1840s a manager called James Henshall actually began as an apprentice at Quarry Bank. His practical knowledge of the Mill and later business education led to him being promoted to run it on a day-to-day basis.

Even so, in 1848, the author William Thackeray's descriptions of workers leaving a Manchester mill included the following statements:

"I stood… and observed the streams of operatives (workers) as they left the mill. The children were ill-looking, small, sickly, barefoot and ill-clad. The men were as pallid and thin as the children. The women were most respectable, though, not a fresh face amongst them caught my eye… There I saw a degenerate race, stunted and enfeebled – children that were never to be healthy adults."

Perhaps conditions from our runaway's time had not improved as much as the various commissioners and inspectors liked to think when, in 1812, Robert Southey the poet had written of a Manchester mill:

"…if Dante had peopled one of his hells with children, here was a scene worthy to have supplied him with new images of torment." (ibid)

More writers of course, like Dickens, Elizabeth Gaskell et al., would continue to write about the poor working conditions endured and about the people subjected to them during the industrialization of Britain for many more decades.

The progress in wealth and status made by apprentices like James Henshall was very much the exception. It has to be remembered that the daily lives of the Greg's own children were quite different to that of the child workers in Quarry Bank Mill. While the Greg's girls stayed at home to be taught by a governess or a tutor, the boys were sent away to expensive schools to learn many languages, mathematics and science. The estate around the mill was where they would spend much of their leisure time; climbing ropes in their own cave; painting and writing; riding on their own model railway; enjoying astronomy from their observatory, and so on. Mill children would be grateful for enough free time to play with roughly made, cheap wooden toys or chanting and signing games; that is if they had been able to stay awake long enough from catching up on their sleep, so much deprived during their many exhausting hours working to produce profitable cotton yarn for their mill masters.

The population of Britain would continue to grow rapidly through the rest of the 19th century and the lower classes would also see improvements in their lives through the many developments in agriculture, transport and industrial technology. Mass-production would bring down the cost of very many household items and ordinary working people would be able to take advantage of the 'new consumerism'. Lives in general would improve with advances in medicine, hygiene and food production; window shopping and marketing goods would become acceptable cultural activities.

We do not know what destiny had in store for our young heroes, Thomas Priestley and Joseph Sefton, but we can hope that things also turned out well for them.

G J Griffiths

Glossary of Words and Terms

Beartown: Congleton
Bob (cash): slang for shilling coin
Bobbin: cotton reel or spindle
Boggart: evil spirit or ghost
Bottle kiln: type of pottery firing oven
Brazier: hot coals holder
Breeches: trousers
Brimstone: sulphur
Canoc: Cannock
Carbolic: disinfectant
Carding: combing to clean cotton, wool
Chenet: Cannock
Chorley (Old): Alderley Edge
Clammins: doors to kilns
Clouts: trousers or clothes
Cobbles: small round stones
Consumption: TB or tuberculosis
Cony: rabbit
Coppice: cleared woodland area
Cotton boll: cotton seed capsule
Crown (cash): five shillings
Cut: canal
Doffing: changing mule spindles
Doss: sleep rough
Dray: cart with no sides
Drover: driver of livestock
Faggot: bundle of sticks
Farthing: one quarter of an old penny
Fustian: thick rough cloth
Gaffer: boss

Gander (take a): look
Gig: light horse carriage
Gruel: very thin watery porridge
Half-crown (cash): two shillings and sixpence
Hanky-panky: improper behaviour
Indenture: formal contract
Jiggered: exhausted
Joshing: playfully teasing
Kickrew: Kidsgrove
Knackers: disposer of animals
Lobscouse or lobby: beef and vegetables stew
Lurcher: greyhound and retriever or collie cross
Nowt: nothing
Nowty: grumpy
Overseer: supervisor
Pease: soaked dried split peas
Physic: medicinal drugs
Piecing: joining broken yarns
Pollard: cut off the top and branches of trees
Pressgang: a group who force others to join army or navy
Privy: a toilet/wc
Saggar: fire clay box to hold pottery wares in kiln
Scavenging: cleaning up of waste cotton
Shellac: resin varnish
Shilling: twelve old pence (five new pence)
Shoddy or short silk etc: cheaper quality fabric
Shuttle: weaving bobbin carrying weft yarn
Silk throwing: winding of yarn onto bobbins
Snap: small lunch or snack
Spinning mule: Crompton's large spinning machine
Tanner (cash): slang for sixpence coin
Taters: potatoes
Tha knowst: you know
Thesen or thysell: yourself
Throstle spinner: a spinning machine
Thrupence or threppence: three (old) pennies
Tod (on his): alone
Tuppence: two (old) pennies
Watling Street: A5 Roman Road
Worsted: smooth woollen cloth

PREVIEW of Mules; Masters & Mud

The sequel to *The Quarry Bank Runaways* is called *Mules; Masters & Mud* and continues the tale of the two apprentices as grown men over three more decades. Here is the Prologue as a short preview for your appreciation.

"The rich man in his castle,
The poor man at his gate,
God made them, high or lowly,
And order'd their estate,"

Mrs Alexander (1818-1895)

"The year's at the spring
And day's at the morn;
Morning's at seven;
The hill-side's dew pearled;
The lark's on the wing;
The snail's on the thorn:
God's in his heaven,
All's right with the world!"

Robert Browning (1812-1889)

MULES; MASTERS & MUD

Prologue

In the year 1806 two boys, Thomas Priestley and Joseph Sefton, were cotton apprentices who ran away from Quarry Bank Mill in Styal, Cheshire. They took about a week to walk to London. Another cotton worker, whose name was James Henshall, had a successful career at the same mill, beginning there also as an apprentice but he became the mill manager from 1847 to 1867. This was not the norm for most apprentices during the Industrial Revolution, far from it. The story of the events that befell Thomas and Joseph, while on their journey to Hackney workhouse in London, concluded with a strong sense of hope. As we are well aware the fates often have a way of confounding things in a way that is usually quite unexpected.

This continuation of their story is about what happened to those boy apprentices over the succeeding few decades, first as young men with hopes, and then later when they're full grown. By the start of the Victorian era the fates and their ambitions had collided. The earlier chapters are about some of the events that occurred along the way adding a little more colour to Thomas' and Joseph's lives and perhaps giving a sense of the difficulties and hurdles that stood in the way of ambitious and determined working class individuals.

These rare, aspirational individuals struggled, not only to physically survive during the Industrial Revolution, but to somehow withstand the oppressively exhausting mental battering that resulted from the daily tedium of long hours working in hard and often dangerous employment. Many of the workers would have commenced their employment of course as indentured children from the age of nine, or even younger. These individuals could be considered the 'lucky' few who may have survived to adulthood – but all too often they were lame or deformed through the abusive treatment and strictures imposed upon them at work.

It is probably worth recalling a sentence that, unfortunately, applied well to the first book entitled *The Quarry Bank Runaways*. That sentence is: "Child apprentices in very many cotton mills continued to be treated like slaves well after the Slave Trade Acts of the 19th century."

Mud larks

CPSIA information can be obtained
at www.ICGtesting.com
Printed in the USA
BVHW041510041019
560259BV00014B/1033/P